MW01136928

Lockhart Brothers: Book One

DEEP DOWN

brenda rothert

*There is greatness deep down
in all of us.*

xo Brenda Rothert

Cover Designer:
Regina Wamba, Mae I Design
www.maeidesign.com

Cover Photo by: Shutterstock

Interior Design and Formatting:
Christine Borgford, Perfectly Publishable
www.perfectlypublishable.com

BOOKS BY BRENDA ROTHERT

NOW SERIES
Now and Then
Now and Again
Now and Forever

FIRE ON ICE SERIES
Bound
Captive
Edge
Release
Drive

ON THE LINE SERIES
Killian
Bennett (coming soon)
Liam (coming soon)

STANDALONES
Unspoken

PART ONE

ONE

Ivy

IT HAPPENED WITHOUT WARNING on a quiet, snowy January day. Or maybe there had been signs that I'd ignored because they were too painful to acknowledge. Either way, the course of my life was changed that day. After it was over I just remember watching the snowflakes through my open bedroom window. Falling silently from the sky, they were the closing curtain on eighteen years of trusting that all people were inherently good.

IT WAS THE FIRST day back from the winter break and I was wrapped up in the excitement that filled the hallways of Lexington High School. There was an unspoken energy circulating around those of us who were seniors.

Home stretch, baby. The last semester of high school is underway. Your future starts now.

And, for me, this new term couldn't end soon enough. My mom's death this past September had plunged me into a deep sadness I still hadn't fully emerged from. Over the course of the past four months I'd gotten good at plastering on a phony smile to let everyone know I'd moved on. Putting this school year behind me would be more sweet than bitter. Sure, I had great friends I'd miss when I went off to college in the fall. And dance team . . . for sure I would miss *that*. Most of all, I would miss my boyfriend Levi, but somehow I knew that once high school was over I really would be able to move on.

A warm, familiar arm wrapping around my waist from behind made me break out in a genuine grin.

"How was your day, baby?" Levi asked, pulling me against his side as we walked down the hall.

"Good. You?"

He shrugged. "Everybody's talking about graduation. It hasn't seemed close until now."

"Did you get those scholarship essays done?"

"Yep." He pulled me a little closer, steering me away from a cluster of loud underclassmen who were about to run me over.

"Am I riding with you today? I can catch a ride home with Sami if you're lifting weights after school."

He leaned down and kissed my temple. "The only weight I'm interested in right now is yours on top of me."

I held back a smile. Our after school make out sessions were one of Levi's favorite things. But between the time off his parents and my dad had taken over the holiday break, we hadn't gotten much time alone.

"I have to start reading for my English project," I said, giving him a warning look.

His expression clouded and he pulled his arm away

2

from me. "Sure. Whatever."

"I don't mean as soon as I get home. I've got an hour or so free."

"How nice." Levi rolled his eyes, refusing to look at me.

"Today's the only day I don't have dance," I said. "And this is a huge project. I'm not losing my 4.0 now. Not after I managed an A in Calc last semester even with everything with my mom."

My voice was thick with emotion. Levi sighed and reached for my hand.

"Sorry," he said. "It's just sometimes it feels like you don't care about anything but school stuff. It's not easy, you know, being with a virgin—"

"Could you say that a little bit louder? I know the halls are crowded and noisy, but there's a chance some-one might have missed it."

"Very funny, Ivy. Everyone knows. There are only a handful of virgins left in our class and we all know who they are."

"That doesn't mean anyone needs to overhear my boyfriend griping about it."

"I'm not griping. I'm just saying that sometimes it seems like we only mess around because *I* want to."

This time it was me sighing with exasperation. He was right—I did sometimes let him feel me up and grind against me through our clothes just to placate him. My mind wandered during those make out sessions. I'd think about my homework, the Stanford campus, dance routines I was working on. Sometimes I thought about my mom. Those were the times I'd cling to Levi and fight back the tears. He always took it as a sign that I was into whatever he was doing, but really I just craved the comfort.

"I want to, okay?' I said with an edge. "But I have a ton of homework. Calc is kicking my butt."

"I'll make it better." Levi winked and returned his arm to my waist. "I know how to take your mind off everything."

We'd made it to the concrete steps outside the school, and I wrapped my coat around me to block out the icy Michigan wind. Levi jogged down the stairs and I rushed to keep up with him. He was still in prime shape from football season. I was in great shape from dance, but I didn't have his long legs and ability to fly down the stairs without tripping.

"My nuts are frozen," he grumbled as we got in his tiny sports car.

I cranked up the heat as he pulled out of the parking lot. When I looked up, my friend Regina was waving wildly from several cars away. I blew her a kiss and waved back.

"Is it true she fucked McAllister over break?" Levi asked.

I shrugged. It was true, from what she'd told me, but she'd asked me not to repeat it.

"So . . ." Levi tapped his fingers on the steering wheel. "We've kinda talked about this, but I haven't officially asked. I'm hoping you'll go to prom with me?"

"Of course I will," I said, smiling at his uncertainty. We'd started dating right before prom last year so this would be our second time going together.

"And, uh . . ." He tapped a little faster. "I mean, rooms will be booking up, so . . . I was thinking of getting us a room at a hotel . . ."

My stomach flipped nervously. In a rare moment of

impulsiveness, I'd suggested to Levi that we could have sex for the first time on prom night. We were both eighteen. We loved each other. And even though I was going to college in California and he was going to a state school here in Michigan, it still felt right.

"Yes," I said. "Go ahead and get one. I'll split the cost with you."

He reached for my hand and squeezed it. "Ivy. I've got the room. I want it to be a special night since it's your first time."

Levi wasn't a virgin. He'd been with three girls already when we'd started dating. And other than the grumbling, he'd been patient.

"Let's go to your house," he said, stroking a thumb across my palm. "My mom's working from home today. I won't stay long since you've got homework."

Had I picked up this morning? I was pretty sure I'd deposited the half dozen empty beer cans dad had left on the counter last night into the trash can. He'd taken up drinking after mom died, and since he mostly did it at home, it wasn't something anyone but me knew about. And I wanted to keep it that way. It would just make people feel sorry for both of us, and I didn't want that.

"Dad's working 'til five," I said.

"I'll be gone long before that. You must know I'm crazy into you since I'm willing to risk making out with a cop's daughter right on his couch."

"I'm eighteen, Levi. I'm pretty sure my dad thinks I'm sleeping with you anyway."

"What?" He gave me a horrified glance.

"He's made comments."

"Oh, shit."

I squeezed his hand reassuringly. "Most eighteen

-year-olds have sex. My parents were nineteen when they got married. And my dad likes you."

"Yeah, but . . ."

"Relax. He'll only shoot you in the leg if he catches us. Nothing fatal."

"That's not funny, Ivy."

I laughed at his nervousness. My dad had never been the intimidating type of police officer. He was laid back and happy most all the time. At least he had been before mom died. Like me, he still seemed to be struggling to find a normal without her in it. And the way he'd started looking at me when he made comments about me and Levi, his eyes dark and his voice sounding almost *jealous,* well . . . that hadn't been the case when Mom was alive.

Levi turned onto my street and I pulled out my phone to check messages. I didn't have much to look at, since most of my friends had been in school with me.

When Levi groaned, I looked up. "What?"

He nodded at my driveway as he slowed his car. "Looks like your dad's not working after all."

I saw my dad's marked squad car and scrunched my face in confusion. Dad never left work early. Was he sick? A wave of unease passed over me. Mom had been fine until suddenly feeling sick one day. A bacterial infection had taken her life in just three short weeks.

"Wanna go park instead?" Levi asked.

"Uh, no. I think I need to go make sure my dad's okay. He's been . . . kind of off lately."

He turned into the driveway, parked and gave me a perfunctory kiss.

"You're worth waiting for," he said, smiling. His compliment aggravated me, because I knew I was worth waiting for and I was tired of being reminded of it like he was some kind of saint for keeping his pants zipped.

"I'm riding with Regina in the morning," I said.

"OK, text me later."

I nodded and stepped out of the car, waving as he backed out of the driveway. I made the trip to our street side mailbox in a hurry, flipping through the stack of bills as I walked up to the garage door keypad and typed in the code.

The 'S' logo on a return address grabbed my attention. Stanford. I'd already been accepted, but every letter from my future school brought on a fresh wave of excitement. I was getting out of Lexington. Hopefully a new place would be a fresh start, without the sadness that followed me everywhere here. And Stanford had been Mom's dream for me.

I tore into the envelope as the garage door creaked its way up.

Dear Miss Gleason,
We are pleased to inform you that you are the recipient of the Thomas and Viola Stringer Memorial Scholarship.

My heart pounded wildly as I read the words which were soon blurred by tears. I'd gotten it. Somehow, I'd gotten an academic scholarship that would fund all tuition, room and board for my freshman year. And, if I got good grades, it was renewable.

I blinked and tears dropped onto my cold cheeks. Dad wouldn't have to work overtime to afford my tuition. That thought had been weighing on my mind and this news made me feel about twenty pounds lighter. Dad would be so proud of me. Finally we had something to celebrate.

Gently, I folded the letter and returned it to its envelope. How would I tell him? Maybe I'd make hamburgers for dinner—his favorite—and then slide the envelope across the table while he was eating.

I couldn't contain myself. I pushed the door open and flew into the house, not sure if I wanted to dance or cry. There was no way I could wait until dinner to tell him. I just hoped I could get the words out without bursting into joyful tears. There had been so many tears for both of us in the past five months, but none had been happy.

"There y'are." Dad's slurred voice sounded from the couch as soon as I walked into the living room. "No romp on the couch with loverboy today, I s'pose?"

I swallowed hard at his bitter tone. There were almost a dozen beer cans on the coffee table in front of him, all with the tops opened. He was drunk, which happened often lately, but never at 3:30 in the afternoon.

"Did you get off work early?" I asked, slipping my backpack off my shoulder and onto the ground. I put my Stanford letter into the front pocket and then stepped forward to gather the empty cans.

"I'm here, right?" he said.

"I thought I'd make hamburgers for dinner."

His hand shot out and locked around my wrist.

"Olivia." His tone was rough with emotion as he said my mother's name. My heart pounded and I felt a whooshing sensation in my ears.

"It's me, Dad. Ivy."

"I know," he said, sounding both confused and disgusted.

The letter was forgotten. Fear swam through my veins as he looked at me. Something was very wrong, and my flight instinct was screaming.

"Go put some lipstick on," he said gruffly.

A wave of nausea rose so powerfully it made me dizzy. Lately, I'd noticed him looking at me differently, but I had told myself it was just my imagination. This was different, though. His dark eyes were cold and unfamiliar.

"I have to go to dance practice," I said, turning toward the door. "I'll be home soon."

I had no idea where I would go. I'd walk somewhere. Call someone for help. I just had to get out of here.

"No." He was off the couch and behind me now. My skin prickled with fear. "Get back here."

"Dad, what—"

His hand wrapped around my wrist again, jerking me into silence. He dragged me, stumbling, toward the hallway that led to my bedroom.

I was going to be sick. I tasted vomit and felt hot tears stinging my eyes. This was worse than any nightmare I'd ever had.

He wasn't a violent man. He'd never laid a hand on me. But I prayed silently that he was about to beat me. It would hurt, but I could survive it. As he tossed me onto the rumpled covers of my bed, I hoped he'd slap me. I wanted him to work out whatever craziness he was feeling any other way than the one I suspected he was thinking of.

"Don't do this," I said, pushing myself away from him with my feet and hands. "You've been drinking, and whatever this—"

"Shut up." His voice was eerily calm as his weight descended on me, pinning me to the bed. "You don't know. I never wanted . . . other women. Only her."

I was crying hard now, terror making me shake from head to toe. "She's gone. And you don't want to do this."

9

"Shut your mouth." He pinned my arms above my head with one hand and worked my jeans open with the other.

Instinct kicked in and I thrashed against him, trying to knee him in the groin. "No! Stop. You can't do this. Stop, Dad."

I couldn't even move him and my struggles seemed to make him even more incensed. He was so much bigger and stronger. Vomit rose up my throat and I swallowed it in my struggle.

"Stop making this hard," he said, my jeans and panties now around my knees. "You give it up to your boyfriend all the time."

His hand was on the zipper of his own pants now, and I kicked my legs in a frantic effort to stop him.

"No! No, no, no. Just let me go. I'll make hamburgers, we'll forget about this," I cried, my voice desperate. "Please."

It was as if he didn't even hear me. He used one leg to hold mine still. The eyes staring down at me were black and unfamiliar. I realized my dad was gone, too. No matter what happened from here, I'd never again see him as the man who had raised me, the man who'd been a devoted husband and father. He and mom had been there, cheering me on, during my swim meets and dance recitals. When I was little, he'd carried me around the house on his shoulders so I could touch the ceiling. Suddenly, he was a stranger to me. And now he was about to ruin me forever.

Survive. Just survive, Ivy.

I turned my head to the side and squeezed my eyes closed. When I was ten I'd been very sick and had had to endure lots of blood work with collapsed veins. My mom had held my hands the whole time, whispering words of comfort in my ear and stroking my hair.

"I'm here, baby."

Her voice echoed in my head as I breathed in and out. A shockwave of pain hit, but I bit down on my lip and reminded myself I could get though anything with my mom beside me.

"Everything's okay."

Breathe in, breathe out.

"Mommy's right here."

Breathe in, breathe out.

"That's my brave girl."

I listened to her, my mind somewhere far away from what was happening in my bedroom.

Then it was over. The weight lifted off my chest and my breath came easier. I wanted to crawl away, run, hide, but I was paralyzed with shock and fear. My father leaned above me, his face a mask of shock and horror.

"Jesus Christ," he whispered, looking at me. "What did I . . ."

I closed my legs and curled into a ball, wrapping my arms around my shaking body.

"Ivy."

I let myself stay in a protective trance, not acknowledging him or my surroundings.

"I didn't mean for that . . ." he slurred. Then, as if the full realization hit him, he seemed to sober up immediately and he added, "You can't tell anyone about this. Not one word. No one would believe you anyway. We're both gonna forget this happened, okay? You just . . . clean up and go make dinner."

He left the room. I wanted to cry, but I couldn't. Instead I pulled my pants up and ran to my bathroom, where I closed the door and turned the lock on the handle. If he really wanted to get in, that lock wouldn't stop him for long, but it made me feel better.

A few minutes later I heard the front door close and then I heard him pull out of the driveway.

I cautiously opened the bathroom door and went back into my room. I pulled up the blinds on the window next to my bed. Then I opened the window, inhaling sharply as a cold winter breeze touched my skin.

My hands shook as I dislodged the screen. I leaned it up against the wall and stared out into the back yard. The swing set I'd played on when I was small was still there, its white and blue paint now faded and rusted in places.

If he came back and touched the door knob, I'd crawl out the window. But for now, I needed the comfort of my bed. I buried myself beneath my purple comforter, tucking it around me. I was cold, scared and completely horrified. I didn't know what to do so I lay in bed looking out the window, watching the snow begin to fall.

I'd just been raped by my own father. He was the only parent I had, and he'd ignored my cries as he hurt me. It was too awful to be real.

Eventually, the tears came and I cried into my pillow until darkness fell over the room. I wanted my mom so much my stomach began to ache. Even when I closed my eyes, sleep was impossible. The icy January air coming in the wide open window had lowered the temperature in the room. I was still shaking, though I didn't know if it was from the cold or from fear.

The Stanford letter, dinner and my homework weren't important anymore. Right now it was all I could do to keep breathing.

TWO

I WAS WRAPPED UP in my covers, wide awake, when I heard the back door close early the next morning. Dad was leaving for work. I waited until I heard his car start and pull out of the driveway before I got out of bed and unlocked my bedroom door.

As soon as I stepped in front of the bathroom mirror, I knew I looked as awful as I felt. The dark circles beneath my eyes stood out on my fair skin. My blue eyes were swollen and rimmed with red. And my long auburn hair was a tangled mess in bad need of a washing.

A shower would help. And hopefully it would ease the pain between my legs. I turned the lock on the bathroom door and cranked the knob on the shower to hot. As steam filled the room, I brushed my teeth.

I couldn't stop looking at the face in the mirror. It looked like me. But something was off. My own reflection felt unfamiliar for the first time in my life. Yesterday morning I'd seen that my hair needed a trim and my lips looked a little dry. Today all I saw was emptiness.

Taking in a deep breath and then letting it out, I pulled

my shirt up over my head and tossed it to the floor. My skin broke out in goose bumps. A cold, exposed feeling wound around me, so strong it was suffocating.

I grabbed my shirt and slipped it back on, wrapping my arms around myself. A shower would probably cleanse away some of the shame I felt right now. I knew that in my head, but I couldn't bring myself to undress for it.

Part of me wanted to take a sick day from school and get back in bed. But the thought of staying here filled me with a sick unease. I'd be terrified every minute that he'd walk in. No, I had to get out of here.

I glanced at the clock and saw that Regina would be picking me up in half an hour. I ran a brush through my hair and covered up my fatigue with makeup. Changing into clean clothes was quick and mechanical. I felt too sick to eat, so I spent ten minutes sitting on the front steps waiting for Regina. It was cold outside, but I had to get away from my bedroom.

Regina's red sports car pulled into the driveway and I got in.

"Hey," she said, turning down the music. "Did you hear about Peyton and Jen?"

I shook my head silently. She launched into a story about Jen's father chasing Peyton out of his house while Peyton was naked. I tuned her out, staring at the passing scenery instead.

The swings at the park I'd played at as a kid swayed slightly in the wind. The park wasn't much—just swings, a couple slides and some monkey bars with peeling red paint. But going there had made for a perfect afternoon when I was little. Now it looked lonely and deserted.

The letter 'r' on the sign for Marla's nails was hanging

upside down, looking like it would fall off at any moment. How long had it been like that?

Even these familiar places seemed off today. I was in a haze, my eyes burning with exhaustion and my pulse racing with nervous worry.

"Ivy?" Regina said, aggravated. "Are you even listening to me?"

"Sorry. I think I'm getting the flu."

"Well, shit. Can you stop breathing in my car? If I miss one more day I have to take finals."

I resumed staring out the window until we pulled into the school parking lot. As soon as we walked in the front door, Regina headed toward a group of our friends. They were laughing and goofing off.

I saw Levi and my stomach turned. The thought of being touched right now was too much.

Without a word to Regina, I turned toward the bathroom and rushed in. Several freshmen were in there putting on makeup and passing a bottle of hair spray around. I bypassed them and went into a stall, sitting down and burying my face in my hands.

How would I get through this day? I knew I couldn't smile, laugh or get within ten feet of Levi. I'd be lucky not to break down crying in class.

The bell rang, and it was all I could do to put one foot in front of the other to get to my locker. I hurried to my first class, not meeting anyone's eyes in an attempt to avoid conversation.

That tactic worked most of the day. If someone spoke to me, I shrugged or told them I was feeling sick. That got me out of dance practice, too.

After a few days, I had no choice but to paste on a smile and act like the Ivy everyone was used to. But inside I was hollowed out. Dancing, joking around and even smiling made me feel like an imposter.

I wanted to be alone. Anytime I was with another person, I was pretending. I couldn't talk about the thing that had taken over my mind not just when I was awake, but in my dreams as well. I woke up every morning sweating and scared. I was suffocating, and acting like a carefree teenager was the hardest thing I'd ever done.

Living at home became a nightmare in itself. Every morning I didn't leave my bedroom until Dad had left for work, and I was in my bedroom with the door locked when he arrived home late every night. I would often hear him stumbling into things after he came inside, so I knew he was spending his evenings at a bar. My concern for him was gone. I was just grateful I didn't have to see him.

Days turned into weeks. The sleepless nights were wearing on me. I'd nodded off in Levi's car on the way home from school one day and he woke me by brushing the hair away from my face.

"No," I said, jerking away from him so hard I knocked my head against the passenger side window.

"Ivy, what's going on with you?" The concern in his voice told me my act was wearing thin.

"Sorry, I was asleep. I didn't realize it was you."

"Who else would it be?"

I sighed deeply. "I'm just stressed."

"You've been saying that for weeks."

"I'm not just saying it. It's the truth."

He shifted in his seat so he was turned toward me. "Something's going on. You either jump or pull away every time I touch you. We haven't done anything but kiss in more than a month."

"You're keeping track?" I snapped. "Is that all I am to you?"

"It didn't used to be like this, Ivy. If there's someone else, just say it."

I gave him back the pissed-off glare he was giving me. "There's no one else."

"Just fucking tell me what's up." He slammed a hand against his steering wheel. "Am I gonna get dumped right before prom?"

Of course, he was more worried about himself than me. Was this a universal trait in men?

"I don't even care about prom," I said. It was the first honest thing I'd said in weeks, and it felt good. "Ask someone else. And you're right—this isn't working anymore."

He narrowed his eyes in confusion. "You're breaking up with me?"

"I guess so."

"You *guess* so? Who the fuck is it, Ivy? You've been cheating on me, haven't you?"

I shook my head and opened the car door once we pulled into my driveway. "No. All I care about is graduating and getting the hell out of here. I'm moving to California as soon as the ceremony is over."

The words had just come out of my mouth without me thinking about it, but I knew as soon as I'd said it that it was a good idea, a really good idea. I'd count the days until May 16 and then I would move to California. I could get a job to meet my expenses until classes started in August.

"So that's it?" Levi said. "All this time and you feel nothing?"

Little did he know that feeling nothing sounded like

a dream come true. All I did anymore was *feel*. Scared, angry, ashamed, worried. Could I ever get to a point where I felt nothing?

"I guess not," I said, getting out of the car. It was the truth; I actually didn't feel much of anything for Levi anymore. And maybe if I tried hard enough, I could stop all the other feelings, too. If I didn't, they were going to drown me.

I SAT ON MY bedroom floor with my back against the door, staring up at the swirling ceiling fan. Even sitting up took energy, so I let myself crumple down onto the worn beige carpet. I'd been so stupid and naïve to think I was at rock bottom. So confident things couldn't get any worse.

But, today, they were ten times worse. I shook my head, wishing for yesterday, when what my father did to me six weeks ago had been my biggest problem.

My period was late. It wasn't something I'd ever kept track of, but I knew I hadn't gotten it since that day. And I knew that day was six weeks and one day ago.

The sense of sickness and dread was almost too much. I'd barely been keeping my head above water, but this? If I was pregnant from my own father . . .

Just the thought sent vomit rushing up my throat. I crawled over to my pink metal trash can, making it just in time.

I wiped my sleeve across my mouth after vomiting, not caring how gross it was. I didn't want to know. The only reason I got out of bed every morning was because I was getting out of here in May. I was going to California to start over in a place that didn't haunt me like my own bedroom now did.

My shame was my secret. I knew what had happened wasn't my fault, but I was still ashamed. If I was pregnant, though, how long would it stay a secret?

The pain and fear were overwhelming. And there was no escape. If I was pregnant, those feelings would follow me to California or anywhere else I went.

I thought about my mom and the way she had clutched my hand when she was sick in the hospital, telling me to be strong. Her pale blue eyes had implored me as she said the words. I promised her I would. I'd thought she'd meant be strong in handling her death, but I now realized she had meant so much more. That promise echoed in my mind now.

The first step was finding out whether I was pregnant or not. That would take strength and resolve. I wanted to stay on the floor, but I thought of my mom and I pulled myself back to a sitting position.

I had to think this through. I couldn't be seen buying a pregnancy test. Everyone knew I was the deputy sheriff's daughter, and the last person I wanted knowing about this was my father.

Reluctantly, I reached for my backpack, fished out my phone and pushed a button to call Regina.

"Hey, what's up?" she said, laughing.

"Um . . . can you come over? I need your help with something."

"Sure, give me half an hour."

I took a deep breath and gathered my courage. "Can you stop somewhere and . . . um . . . get a pregnancy test? I'll pay you back."

There was a pause on the other end of the phone.

"Sure. I'll be there as soon as I can."

I paced from the kitchen to the living room while I waited for Regina to arrive. Every time I passed the family photo in the hallway, I glanced over at my mom's smiling face. What would she think of me right now? She'd hug me and say all the right things, but what would she feel in her heart?

Surely she'd feel what I did. *Disgust.* What my dad did to me was his fault, not mine, but still. Still. The possibility I was pregnant with my own father's child was disgusting to me.

My lip quivered and I wiped the tears from my cheeks. I'd thought my biggest stress in my last semester of high school would be maintaining my Calculus grade. That didn't even compare to this.

A knock at the door made my stomach turn with revulsion and anxiety. When I opened it, Regina stood on the front step grinning at me.

"What the hell, Ivy?" she said, stepping inside. "You said you never gave it up to Levi. Is this why you guys broke up? Does he know?"

I answered her question with one of my own, "Did you bring it?"

She reached into her bag and pulled out a plastic sack, handing it to me.

"Thanks," I said weakly. "You don't have to stay."

"Like hell. I'm staying. Let's open that bitch so you can pee on it."

I read the instructions, drowning out her questions about who and when and why. She followed me into the bathroom.

"Ivy." She grabbed my arm. "It is Levi's, right? Or . . . ?"

"Look, I have to focus on this right now."

"Sure, sure. Go ahead."

I peed on the stick and then sat on the lid of the toilet seat to wait, burying my head in my hands.

One line, not pregnant. Two lines, pregnant. One line, and I can get through this. Two lines, and I don't know if I can be strong enough to face the future. One line, and my father did something terrible to me. Two lines, and I'm in a world of trouble.

My hand shook as I picked up the stick to look at the results. Regina was looking over my shoulder.

"Two lines?" she said. "What's that mean?"

I let the stick fall to the floor. It meant the end of everything.

Regina's eyes widened and she bit her lip in an attempt to conceal her smile.

"Oh my God, Ivy. Oh. My. God. What are you going to do? Is it Levi's?"

"I just . . . I don't . . ." The tears came hard and fast. "Can you please not tell anyone about this, Regina? *Please.* I need some time to . . ."

"Are you gonna get an abortion?"

I reached for the sink counter to brace myself against the dizziness. "I need to lay down. I'm sorry, you have to go. I'll pay you back . . . later."

She waved a hand. "Don't worry about it. Text me later, OK?"

"Sure."

I followed her to the door and opened it for her.

"Are you gonna tell Levi?" she asked again.

"I can't . . . talk about this right now. I'll talk to you later."

I closed the door behind her, covering my mouth to

stifle a sob. Instinct drove me toward my bedroom. This time, I didn't look over at my mom's picture in the hallway. I couldn't stand to see it right now.

Numbness set in. I couldn't think about anything. I locked my bedroom door, buried myself under my covers and let exhaustion swallow me.

THREE

NO ONE SPOKE TO me at school the next morning, but everyone was sure looking at me. And they weren't the kind of glances I was used to. These looks were similar to Regina's: shocked amusement.

Lunch was the worst. Instead of sitting with friends at my usual table, I sat in a chair in the student lounge and read a book while forcing myself to eat a grilled chicken sandwich. Not eating wasn't an option anymore. The baby inside me deserved to grow and be healthy. Now that I knew the truth, in my mind, it was no different than holding a newborn in my arms. I'd cradle that baby, feed it and keep it warm. I was holding this baby inside me, and I would care for it.

"Hey," a deep male voice said. I looked up from my paperback. It was John McGinnis. He played football with Levi. In true jock fashion he wore his letterman jacket even though it wasn't cold inside the school. "I heard you're knocked up. That true?"

What a jerk. I sighed deeply. Had I really thought Regina would keep things quiet? Though I had my

23

suspicions about how, overnight, I had turned into a pariah at Lexington High School, this question from McGinnis confirmed it.

"Is it any business of yours?" I asked.

He shrugged. "Levi said he never fucked you. Did you cheat on him?"

"Again, John—not your business. Go away. I'm kind of in the middle of something here."

"You're a little whore. He never messed around on you. Guy had to have the bluest balls ever, but he never fucked around. And you let some other guy pop your cherry?"

My cheeks burned with anger and embarrassment. I looked down at my book, ignoring him. After a few seconds, he walked away. People around me stared and whispered.

How many times since I started high school had I seen someone else treated badly? Had I ever been one of the people whispering?

I had. I wasn't like Regina, who spread gossip around for fun, but I'd sure listened to my fair share and sometimes I'd reacted. I'd listened to talk that was none of my business. And now I was finding out how it felt to be on the other end.

When I'd been upset about high school drama in the past, my mom had always reminded me that it would pass and not to get too caught up in it. But this wouldn't pass. Not now, not ever. I was irrevocably changed.

The next couple of weeks passed in a fog. I couldn't think past whatever day it was. Survival was all I could manage and I focused on schoolwork and worried about what the future held for me. And sometimes, lots of times, I was sure I couldn't hold on any longer.

There was no escape. Even when I slept, it was fitful. When I dreamed, it was usually about my father's crushing weight on top of me. The horror never faded. Every night, my subconscious experienced it anew.

Some nights I dreamed about my mom. Usually, every time I dreamed about her, she'd be in a hospital bed near death. But recently I saw the healthy, vibrant woman she'd been before getting sick. I'd hold on tightly and feel my pain pouring out as she smoothed a hand over my hair.

Waking up from those dreams was just as bad as waking up from the ones about my dad. Reality packed a cruel punch.

I'd started walking to school. Initially, I'd had no choice because Regina didn't want to be seen with me anymore, so I didn't have a ride. But it wasn't so bad. The first few breaths of brisk winter air in the morning were the best part of my day. Walking allowed me to be alone. I was free from the stares and whispers. Free from the sick worry of being in the same house as my dad.

Sometimes I thought walking might be my salvation. When I didn't think I could go on with my life anymore, I didn't consider a violent death. I just imagined walking and never stopping. Eventually I'd find a cliff and walk right over the edge.

If it was just me, I'd end the pain of my existence. But thinking of the baby growing inside me always ended those thoughts. My baby didn't deserve that.

I'd reached the end of a particularly bad day at school and was walking aimlessly. Tiny snowflakes flew around in the biting winter air, but I hardly felt the cold. I was bundled in a winter parka and lost in my thoughts.

Today I'd eaten lunch in a closed bathroom stall at

school to avoid the stares. And instead I got to listen to Mandy Barton telling two other girls that she'd slept with Levi last night to comfort him over what his slutty girl-friend had done to him. They'd speculated about who the father of my child was, eventually deciding on Mr. Schultz, a teacher and coach at my school whom I'd never even spoken to.

I was on the outskirts of our small city, walking past a rusted, abandoned factory, when a car slowed to a stop nearby. I turned to see a marked police car. A familiar sick taste rose in my throat. My dad was giving me a puzzled glance from a rolled down window, his elbow resting on the door.

"Ivy, what are you doing out here? It's the dead of winter and you're miles from home."

"What are *you* doing here? Are you following me?" My icy tone was challenging. What was there to be afraid of now? He'd stolen the vulnerable, trusting part of me. He'd shown me that there was no one in my life I could count on.

"I was on patrol and I saw you," he said, glaring at me. "Get in the car and I'll drive you home. We need to talk."

"*Talk?* Is that code?" I spat out bitterly.

His face was a mix of contrition and anger. "Ivy. Let's not do this. Get in the car."

"No."

"What's this I hear about you being pregnant? Is it true?"

A powerful wave of nausea swept through me. He didn't deserve to know, and he certainly didn't deserve to ask me about it.

"Leave me alone."

"I can help, Ivy. We'll get it taken care of. Come on."

I turned to face the car. "Go away. I don't want your help. I don't want to be around you."

His face fell. The father who had always looked strong and handsome to me now looked tired and pathetic. He nodded and turned the car around, peeling away from the gravel lot of the old factory.

Darkness came early in the winter months. The sun was setting and my hands were getting numb from the cold, so I headed back toward town. I didn't have a lot of money, but I had several hundred dollars in my savings account. I'd earned that money babysitting last summer, and I decided to use a little of it on a room at a small motel.

The floral bedspread in the room was old and scratchy. I didn't have a change of clothes or a toothbrush. But it was warm and safe. Too worn out to worry anymore, I once again sought comfort in the warmth of the covers.

AT SCHOOL THE NEXT morning, I was packing my things up slowly after my Advanced Chem class. It was the last period before lunch, and I was in no hurry to get there. Actually, I was considering lunch in the bathroom again. That half hour of not being stared at like a freak would give me the mental energy to finish this day.

"Ivy?"

My teacher Miss Byerly approached and leaned on the empty desk next to me. I made eye contact to acknowledge her.

"I don't want to intrude, but . . . I'm concerned about you," she said.

"I'm okay."

The classroom had emptied, and Miss Byerly and I looked at each other in silence for a few seconds.

"You're not okay," she said softly. "And I just can't stand to see you like this anymore. I want you to know you're not alone. I see you sitting in class every day and walking through the halls, and you look like a ghost of the girl I used to see."

I'd never had a personal conversation with Miss Byerly, but the sincerity in her voice reached something inside me. I looked down at the desk I sat in, tears blurring the scratched wood surface.

"You can talk to me, Ivy," she said, bending down near the ground and putting a hand on my back. "But you don't have to. If there's something you need—anything at all—just say so. If you want to hang out in here over lunch, or if you need a ride somewhere—"

"I'm pregnant." My voice shook as I spoke the words for the first time. "You know that, right?"

"I've heard that, yes," she said, looking me straight in the eye.

I took in a deep breath and let it out; relieved I'd finally spoken the truth to someone. Everyone knew, but there was something liberating about owning it.

"Do you have anyone there for you?" Miss Byerly asked, her hand now rubbing a slow circle on my back. "I know you just lost your mom over the summer."

I shrugged silently.

"And your dad? Is he upset with you?"

My throat tightened uncomfortably. I couldn't speak, so I squeezed my eyes shut and tried to force away the image of him.

"When I say I'm here, I mean it, Ivy. If you need

someone to take you to the doctor, or a place to stay—"

"I do need a place to stay." The words tumbled out in a hopeful rush.

Miss Byerly's soft hazel eyes hardened a little. "What's going on with your dad, Ivy? Is there something I should know?"

I shook my head, my heart pounding wildly. "Never mind." I wiped my cheeks and gathered my things, standing up.

"No." She stood too. "I don't want . . . I mean, if you don't want to talk about it, it's okay. And I'd love to have you stay with me."

"Oh, I didn't mean that. You don't have to . . ." I took another deep breath. "I just meant if maybe you could help me find a room somewhere. Isn't there a shelter at the Methodist church?"

"Ivy, you're staying with me, and not another word about it. Are you eighteen?"

I nodded.

"Then come down to my room when school lets out," Miss Byerly said. "We'll go to your house and pick up a few things."

My shoulders sagged with relief. I wouldn't have to worry when I closed my eyes in bed at night that I'd wake up to the sound of my dad trying to get in my bedroom door. I'd take a few things that were important to me— the butterfly necklace my mom gave me for my sixteenth birthday, photos of me and her, my clothes. I didn't want most of the stuff from my bedroom. That place was ruined for me. I wanted to escape it and never go back.

Miss Byerly closed the door to her classroom and gestured to her small metal desk.

"I'll pull up a chair and we can have lunch at my

desk if that's okay. I've got a chicken salad sandwich and homemade cookies, and I have plenty to share."

"Okay. Thank you, Miss Byerly."

"Call me April unless we're in class."

April Byerly was a young teacher with long curly brown hair and a pretty smile. I'd heard she dated Mr. Schultz, the teacher who was rumored to be the father of my baby. My cheeks burned as I remembered hearing the girls laughing about it in the bathroom.

I sat down in the chair April had pulled up to one side of her desk.

"Um, you know . . . I mean, I want to say that I've never even spoken to Mr. Schultz. People are saying that he and I . . . that's only a rumor and I have no idea how it started."

She gave me a sympathetic smile and passed me half of her sandwich.

"I didn't give it a second thought, Ivy. Matt and I went out a couple times earlier this year, but it wasn't a love connection for either of us. I know he's a good guy, though. He wouldn't abuse the teacher-student relationship in any way."

"Good. I'm glad you know that. And . . . are you sure you have room for me at your place?"

"I've got a guest room in need of a guest. So, have you been to the doctor yet? And are you taking prenatal vitamins?"

"No. I'm doing my best to eat healthy. No soda or anything like that."

"We'll stop for vitamins on the way home later. And I can set up a doctor appointment for you."

"Thank you."

"I'm not asking anything specific here, Ivy, so don't

take this that way. Is the baby's father part of your life?"

I shook my head adamantly. "I'm on my own now. It's just me."

April opened her mouth to speak and then closed it again.

"What is it?" I asked.

She sighed and bit her lip, looking unsure. "I don't want to overstep. I just want to make sure you know you've got options. If money is an issue—"

"Do you mean abortion?"

She gave a small nod of acknowledgement. "I know this is a difficult, overwhelming time for you. I don't want to make it worse. But do what's best for you, Ivy. No one but you knows what that is. Maybe you aren't even sure right now."

"I got a full scholarship to Stanford," I said softly. "You're the only person I've told about that."

April's face broke into an excited grin.

"Ivy! What an accomplishment. That's amazing. Congratulations!"

"Thanks. Please don't tell anyone, because I'm turning it down."

Her happy expression morphed into one of concern. "You don't have to decide that right now. Take some time—"

"I already know. I can't take a baby to Stanford. There's no way."

April brushed the crumbs from her hands and passed me a chocolate chip cookie. "You have options, though."

I smiled, grateful to be talking about this with someone. "Before my mom had me, she had two miscarriages. When she was so sick and the doctors said she might not make it, she . . ." I cleared my throat, the image of my mom in the hospital bed still bringing me to tears. "She got this warm, happy look in her eyes when I was holding her hand and she said she knew it was the end. That she loved me and wanted to stay with me, but it wasn't meant to be. And that she'd finally get to meet her other two babies."

"Oh, Ivy." Tears shone in April's eyes, too.

"She loved those babies. And I love mine. I don't judge people who make other decisions but, for me, there is no decision. I wasn't planning on being a parent yet, but I'm going to be, and I'll never be a parent who hurts my child."

April sighed deeply. "My heart feels heavy, Ivy. I know enough about you to know something's not right. Don't be afraid to speak the truth. No matter what, no matter who."

"I just want to move forward. And you're helping me do that."

We switched to lighter talk about music and the weather. But in the back of my mind, I was still thinking about our earlier conversation.

As much as I wanted my dad to answer for what he did, I couldn't expose myself to the shame of everyone knowing the truth. Only he and I knew what had happened between us, and only I knew about the pregnancy. And I planned to keep it that way.

FOUR

AFTER MOVING IN WITH April, I found my way out from under the dark cloud I'd been living under. I could sleep peacefully at night. I still had the dreams, but they rarely woke me up. Her tiny guest room with a single bed and desk was my little slice of heaven. I was safe there.

I'd left my dad a one line note telling him I was moving out. I put my cell phone next to the note with all the contacts deleted, both because I no longer wanted the phone he was paying for and because I didn't want him to have a way to reach me.

April would always greet me with a good morning when I wandered into her kitchen after my shower. She'd ask me how my day was shaping up and we'd talk about hers. We'd watch movies and go grocery shopping together. She went to my doctor's appointments with me and she was an amazing support. Having her in my life had helped me banish the thought of walking off a cliff.

Even school felt survivable now. I had lunch in April's classroom every day, rode home with her after school and brushed off the rumors that I'd moved in with her because of our lesbian relationship.

My only invite to prom was from an asshole on the football team who asked in the middle of English class if I'd go with him so he could get laid with no fear of getting me pregnant. I was just two months away from graduation, and though I told myself I could get through anything at this point, the snickers from people whom I used to think were friends still burned.

For prom night, April and I wore the circa-1985 taffeta gowns we'd bought from a secondhand store. She gave me a teased side ponytail and I gave her spiky bangs. We put on frosty pink lipstick and dark blue eyeshadow, posed for pictures in her living room and then watched *Pretty in Pink*.

"This is better than my actual prom was," she said, arching her brows and nodding seriously.

I burst out laughing. "It's hard to take you seriously with your bangs five inches in the air."

"I wish I'd grown up in the eighties. My prom was in 2005 and it was all about how much skin the girls could show."

"What was your dress like?"

She smiled sheepishly. "Uh . . . I wore a strapless blue dress."

"Sounds modest." I elbowed her as we both laughed.

She tipped the fancy bottle of sparkling apple juice we were sharing and took a swig, passing it to me.

"I was supposed to have sex for the first time tonight," I said, clutching the bottle as I thought about the prom night that wasn't meant to be. "With Levi."

"I'm sorry," April said, wrapping her arm around my shoulders. "You've got that sad look in your eyes again."

"Sometimes things don't go as planned." I smiled

weakly.

"So true. I wish I hadn't gotten the Seattle job now. I'd really like to be here to help you and the baby. Are you sure you won't consider moving with me?"

I shook my head. April had found out last week that she'd gotten a job she'd interviewed for a month ago and figured she was a long shot for. It was a great opportunity for her but it meant she was moving at the end of the school year.

Which meant I was moving, too.

"I want to start over somewhere new," I said. "I'm twenty percent scared and eighty percent excited about it."

"Well, you're one hundred percent amazing, Ivy. You've got more strength than a lot of people twice your age. And maybe you'll meet your Blane in this new place."

I smiled at her reference to the movie we'd just watched. "That's not what I want. I just want a quiet place where I can raise my baby and be anonymous."

"If anyone deserves to find that place, it's you."

I SET OFF IN search of my new place the morning after graduation. I'd walked across the stage, which hadn't been all that scary since April was the one standing next to the principal handing out diplomas. I'd kept a hand on my slightly rounded belly and my eyes on April the entire time. My gut told me my father wasn't watching the graduation ceremony from the football stadium's bleachers, and I didn't have any other family to speak of.

April had taken me out to dinner after the ceremony and given me the keys to her 2007 Honda Accord, telling me it was mine now. We'd gone back and forth for several minutes—me crying while saying I couldn't accept it and her saying I had to. I'd been planning to take the bus out of town. A car of my own that was a tangible reminder of April changed my feelings about the trip. Now I was fifty percent scared and fifty percent excited.

We both cried while saying our goodbyes. April tearfully assured me she was going shopping that day for a car fit for a single Seattle woman.

"I can never thank you enough for what you've done for me," I said, holding her close.

"I've loved having you here, Ivy. I told you my guest room needed a guest, and you were the perfect one."

"I'm not talking about the room." I burst into tears again.

"Alright, you," she said, pulling away and wiping my tears away with her thumb. "Go find where you're meant to be. And let me know when you get there."

"I don't have a phone anymore, and I can't afford one."

"Find a payphone. Borrow someone's phone. Go to the library and email me from a computer. You stay in touch with me, Ivy. I mean it."

"I will." I covered my red, swollen eyes with my sunglasses and got into the car.

Seeing April waving goodbye made me cry some more, but once she was out of sight, I turned on some music and let the sense of freedom wash over me.

This was the most exciting thing I'd ever done. No map and no plan. I was just driving and I planned to stop when I found a place that seemed right. Leaving Lexington behind was a physical relief. I hoped the shame and bad memories wouldn't follow me.

I stopped in Indiana to fill up with gas and get something to eat and by afternoon I was in Illinois. The roads weren't busy and I just kept driving, putting Lexington well and truly in my rear view mirror. When I crossed into Missouri I was surprised at how many miles I had traveled and I was tired, but I felt good. The sun was just starting to go down and I was keeping my eyes open in hopes of coming across a cheap motel for the night. And then, as if by providence, a road sign caught my eye.

Lovely — 14 miles

A town called Lovely? I'd never heard of the place but I was intrigued enough to investigate. When I reached the turn-off, I followed the signs directing me to "Beautiful Downtown Lovely." The downtown was built on a square and brick streets surrounded the square's center, which had bright green grass, colorful flowers and a wooden gazebo.

It was quaint and charming. Nice. But was it my future home? I pulled into a parking place and considered my options. I could always find a motel here and explore Lovely tomorrow. Movement near a flower basket that was hung on an old-fashioned black iron light post caught my eye. A bright blue butterfly landed on the greenery.

My breath caught in my chest. My mom had loved butterflies. This was the sign I needed. I determined right then and there that I'd try to make a life for me and my baby right here—in Lovely, Missouri.

LESS THAN A WEEK after arriving in Lovely I'd found a place to live. My new home had a combination kitchen/living room, a bedroom and a small bathroom. The landlord had rented it to me without a deposit since it was a mess and I agreed to clean it up before moving in. Two full days of scrubbing, carpet shampooing and painting had transformed it. I didn't have furniture, but I had a place that was all mine. The furniture would come later.

As I looked out the window at the cornfield that bordered the property, I heard the rumble of a train punctuated by the burst of its blowing whistle. The tracks were only about a quarter of a mile from my efficiency apartment–just another reason for the bargain rent of $250 a month.

For now, I was focused on finding a job. I'd filled out applications all day yesterday. Lovely wasn't a big town, and I hoped I'd find enough places that were accepting resumes. I planned to hit the pavement again today.

I had less than fifty dollars left. I was trying to eat as cheaply as I could while still nourishing my growing baby. A bag of apples from the local grocery store had set me back more than five bucks yesterday. One of those apples and some peanut butter had been my dinner last night after a full day of job hunting.

It was less than a mile from my apartment to Lovely's downtown, so I packed an apple for lunch and decided to walk into town. I planned to splurge on breakfast at the diner I'd walked past several times yesterday during my job search.

About ten minutes later the diner came into view. An unlit neon sign for 'Gene's Diner' hung in the front window and a buzz of activity greeted me when I walked in. Several heads turned in my direction when I walked in. The regulars were giving me a friendly once over.

All the tables were filled, so I crossed the black and white checkered floor and slid onto a stool at the counter.

The day's specials were written out on a chalkboard. Two eggs, two pieces of toast and two pancakes for $3.99? Sold.

"Hi, hon," a middle-aged woman greeted me, stopping for just a beat. "Be right with you." She flew past with a platter in hand, raising it into the air just in time to avoid running into another waitress.

Gene's was filled with lots of gray-haired women, and men wearing ball caps with seed companies or tractor logos stamped on the front. I was definitely the youngest person here.

Five minutes later, the woman who had greeted me was back, pad in hand. "Sorry, hon. We're short on help. What can I get you?"

My ears perked up. "Short on help? I'm looking for a job."

She scanned me quickly. "How old are you?"

"Eighteen. Turning nineteen in a few months."

"Any waitressing experience?"

"No, but I'm a fast learner and a hard worker."

She shook her head. "This place is a zoo every morning. It's no place to learn how to waitress."

"If I could just talk to the owner—"

"You are. I'm Margie. My husband Gene and I are the owners."

Her sharp tone told me that I was at Strike Two.

"Of course," I said. "I really need a job. I promise if you just give me a chance, you won't be sorry."

"You from Lovely? I don't recognize you."

"No, ma'am. I just moved to Lovely recently." I held out my hand. "I'm Ivy Gleason."

She eyed me silently, not shaking my hand.

"I just need a chance," I said, my voice unsteady. I

cleared my throat. "I'll learn fast and work hard."

Margie looked to be around fifty, and I could tell she was a practical woman. Her light brown hair was cut short and she didn't wear any makeup. Her lips thinned as she pressed them together, considering.

"You'd have to work early," she said. "Five am to one pm. And two of your days would be on the weekend."

"Sounds perfect. I'm a morning person."

Her skeptical look faded. "Okay, Ivy. We'll try it. We could sure use a fresh young face around here."

I wanted to leap off the stool and hug her, but I contained myself and settled for a smile. "When can I start?"

"Tomorrow? Can you come back at two this afternoon and we'll do the paperwork?"

"I'll be here. Thank you, Margie. I won't let you down."

"Well, employees eat free, so how about some breakfast?"

My stomach rumbled with approval. "I'd love some. The special would be great. Eggs over medium and wheat toast. And some orange juice."

She scrawled my order in her notepad and set off again.

When I returned that afternoon, Margie took me back to the kitchen to meet Gene. He was a tall, lanky black man with a warm smile. When Margie introduced us, he smiled, nodded and grabbed the bill of his baseball cap, tipping it down just a bit in a greeting.

"Do we have enough eggs to get through tomorrow?" Margie asked her husband.

"Reckon we do," he said, not looking up from the grill he was scraping clean.

"Our deliveries have been off a few times lately,"

she said, looking at me. "They shorted us on eggs and brought us too much butter."

"Oh, that doesn't sound good," I said, although I was pretty sure Margie and Gene wouldn't let a problem like that slow them down.

"Let's go sit in the office in the back and get your paperwork filled out. Just get a drink if you . . ." Her voice trailed off and when I turned to see why, she was staring at my midsection. "Are you pregnant?"

My hand instinctively went to my slightly swollen belly. "Yes, I am."

She sighed deeply and folded her arms across her ample chest. "If you've got a boyfriend who thinks he can sit in our restaurant all day and visit with you, this ain't gonna work out."

"I don't have a boyfriend. It's just me. Me and my baby, that is." I rubbed my tiny bump. "Besides my landlord and the lady at the grocery store, you're the only people I've spoken to in Lovely."

"Are you just passing through? Planning to leave soon?"

"Margie," Gene said. "You need the help." He'd obviously overheard our conversation.

Margie pursed her lips and turned to lead me back to the office. I turned to give Gene a grateful glance, but he was absorbed in cleaning the grill. The paperwork was quick and easy and Margie was really nice. I was relieved to have a job. I'd work my tail off to prove to them that they had done the right thing in taking a chance on me.

Later that night, excited anticipation made it hard to sleep. I thought about what to wear, and when to arrive, and when I would receive my first paycheck. I must've exhausted myself because the next thing I knew it was 4 am.

But by noon that day I knew I'd have no trouble sleeping in the future. I'd been in motion since five am. Margie didn't take it easy on me because I was new, or because I was pregnant, and neither did the customers. I was sweaty, frazzled and exhausted by the end of my shift. But I had $52 in tips in my pocket, and that felt good. I ate a plate of food before leaving, hardly even tasting it, and then I went straight home to bed.

That was how my weekdays went for the next five months. On my days off I grocery shopped, hit all the local garage sales to furnish my apartment, and went to the library. I would always take a book with me when I did my laundry at the Lovely Tub-o-Suds.

I was two days from my due date when a contraction woke me up at three am one late September morning. I called Margie so I could leave a message that I wouldn't be in because I was going to the hospital. Even though it was the middle of the night she answered the call.

"Hello?" she said in a groggy tone.

"Margie, it's Ivy. I'm sorry I woke you. I just wanted to tell you that I won't . . . ah . . . hang on."

I gritted my teeth through the pain of the contraction.

"Are you in labor?" Margie cried, wide awake now.

"I think so."

"I'll be right there to pick you up."

"Just meet me there. I can drive myself."

"Are you crazy? I'll be there in five minutes, Ivy. Sit tight."

It was the scariest, most painful and amazing day of my life. Margie stayed with me through the nine hour labor, telling the nurses to "get their asses in gear" when I needed pain medication. She put cold cloths on my forehead, commiserated with me and told me a hundred times that I could do this.

And, somehow, I did. My exhausted tears became joyful when a nurse put my newborn son in my arms. He was tiny and wrinkly and completely perfect.

I longed for my mom more than ever. She would have loved her grandson as fully and immediately as I did. But as much as I missed her, I was grateful to have a family again.

"It's just us," I whispered to the warm bundle in my arms. "It's you and me against the world, Noah."

PART TWO

THREE YEARS LATER

FIVE

Reed

LOVELY HADN'T CHANGED SINCE I'd been away, but I sure had. While I'd enjoyed my life in the big city of St. Louis, it had given me a new appreciation for my hometown and I was beginning to realize it was the small things that were making the biggest impact on me. In high school, my favorite place to get a sandwich after high school basketball games was the Corner Deli. It was still there on the corner and it still had colorful painted ads on the windows, many of which were wrought with misspellings.

The deli owner, Mack, wasn't much for spelling, but he made a hell of a sandwich and I was here to get four orders of my favorite menu item—the signature Mack Attack.

Mack was working the front counter when I walked in. I hadn't seen him in years, but he pretty much looked the same. His belly was a little bigger, his hairline was a little further back and his face was a little more wrinkled.

"What's it gonna be?" he asked when I got to the front of the line.

I opened my mouth to order but he cut me off.

"You one of the Lockhart boys?"

"Yes, sir."

"Which one? I know you ain't the surgeon 'cause he took out my gallbladder a couple years ago and he's older than you. Tall son of a gun like you, though. How many of you boys are there, anyway?"

"Five."

"Huh. One of your brothers is the accountant, right?"

"That's Austin."

His eyes widened and he hiked his brows up. "You the one that got left at the altar?"

I cringed inwardly. "Yep, that's me. I'm Reed."

"That was a hell of a thing. What kind of a woman leaves a Lockhart at the altar?"

"Well, it was five years ago. We were both fresh out of college. I think we've both moved on."

I scanned the menu, hoping he'd get the hint that I wanted to order.

"Did ya at least get the ring back?" Mack asked.

"I didn't want it back."

"So which one are you? The youngest?"

I exhaled with aggravation. "I'm the next to youngest."

"You here visiting your folks?"

"I'm moving back to Lovely, actually. I'm an attorney and I'm joining my dad's practice."

Mack smiled his approval. "Tall, handsome guy like you who's an attorney? You'll snag some nice Lovely girl and have a house full of kids in no time."

This guy couldn't take a hint, so I decided to end the

conversation on my own. "Can I get four Mack Attacks with pickles and chips? And four bottles of water."

"You got it. Where you movin' to?"

"The apartment above the office."

"We're practically neighbors! Hey, maybe I can get your advice on a parking situation I'm having."

"Uh . . . I'm not familiar with Lovely's codes. I really couldn't give you any legal advice on that."

Mack grunted and turned to pass my order through an open window to the kitchen. I scrubbed a hand over my face and left the counter to wait at one of the tables, hoping that would keep Mack from striking up another conversation.

When my order was done, I took it back to my new place, jogging down the alley and up the wood staircase in the back of the brick building.

My parents and one of my older brothers, Austin, were all unpacking boxes in my new living room. My black lab Snoop ran toward me as soon as I walked in, dragging a piece of brown packing paper in his mouth.

"Hey, buddy," I said, setting the food down on the counter so I could scratch his ears. "You like our new place?"

"We may have to eat around the coffee table," my mom said. "The kitchen table has boxes of dishes on it."

"You guys don't have to stay and work here all day," I said. "I can get all this unpacked."

"Nonsense." Mom furrowed her brow. "My fourth son is back home for good. I want to help you settle in."

Austin was flipping through one of my old Lovely High School yearbooks. Once Mom and Dad had moved out of earshot, he spoke in a low tone. "Did you know Meredith moved back?"

"No."

"Yep. Guess it didn't work out with her and the new guy."

I grunted dismissively. I'd heard from friends that my ex-fiancée got married a month after she called off our wedding.

"She joined Mom's knitting club even though Mom's not her biggest fan. I was over at Mom and Dad's house with Hannah last time they did the knitting thing and I heard Meredith getting all excited when she found out you were moving back."

"Jesus, man. You go to knitting club with your wife? How pussy-whipped are you?"

My brother shoved my shoulder. "I just went to hang out at Mom and Dad's. I drank beer and talked to Dad the whole time."

"Or did you knit a pink sack for Hannah to carry your balls around in?"

Austin glanced over his shoulder, checking to see if Mom was within earshot. "Fuck you," he said in a low tone after he saw that she was in the kitchen.

"With a ribbon to tie it shut?" I continued. "Bet that bag's in her purse right now."

"Hannah's not like that, asshole."

"I didn't say Hannah's like that. Marriage is like that. There's no way you get to play as much basketball as you used to. Or go have a beer anytime you want. Or take a week long hunting trip if you feel like it."

"We've got a two-year-old and Hannah's pregnant. My life's not all about me anymore."

I gave him an apologetic glance. "I know. And I know you're happy. I hope to have what you do when I get older."

"You're only twenty seven. There's no hurry."

"You were younger than that when you got married."

Austin smiled. "Yeah. But I knew Hannah was the one. You should never get married because you think you've reached an age where you're supposed to. Otherwise you might end up like Kyle."

A few seconds of silence lapsed as we both thought about our oldest brother. He'd married his high school sweetheart, Kim, right after they'd graduated. She'd insisted that if she was going to stick by him through his college and med school years, they needed to be married. And now, seventeen years later, none of us envied Kyle's marriage. The tension between him and Kim was obvious. She seemed resentful, but he didn't seem to care anymore.

I SPENT THE REST of the weekend unpacking and catching up with my family and a few friends from high school. I'd thought I was leaving Lovely for good when I went away to college and then to law school. But the place looked different when seen though adult eyes. The small-town feel I'd wanted to get away from as a teenager didn't seem so bad now.

My first morning at Dad's office was busy. It was full of clients and walk-ins who wanted to drop in and meet me or see me again. My kindergarten and fifth grade teachers were included in the parade of people who came through. Seeing everyone reminded me that I was home again.

"Is there a special lady in your life?" Dad's client Mrs. Lovitz asked as she embraced me in our office lobby.

She was a wiry older woman with a helmet of gray powder-scented curls. Lena, our receptionist, swiveled her head in my direction. She was Meredith's older sister, so I'd have to watch what I said around her.

"No, I'm still holding out hope for you, Mrs. Lovitz," I said, grinning.

She laughed and laid her bony hand on my chest. "Such fit bodies on all you Lockhart boys."

Dad was giving me an amused glance from the doorway of his office.

"I'm ready for you, Mrs. Lovitz," he said, saving me. Mrs. Lovitz squeezed my pecs before walking away.

Dad closed the door to his office and Lena laughed from her desk. "She's been lonely since Mr. Lovitz passed away. So, you aren't seeing anyone?"

"I don't have the time or the interest. I'll be working, playing basketball or boxing in all my free time."

"You still box with your brothers?"

"Who else?" I said, smirking. "There's no one else I'd rather punch in the face."

On cue, Austin walked in the front door.

"I heard a nasty rumor that the best looking Lockhart boy is back in town but, the thing is, I never moved away," he said to Lena.

"You already peaked, man," I said. "You're an old married guy in your thirties. Plus, I'm taller."

He scowled at me. "By an inch. Let's go get lunch. I'm starving."

"You burn lots of calories punching buttons on your calculator?"

"My day starts at six am, not nine like you lazy attorneys."

"Let me get my jacket and we can go."

Downtown Lovely was decorated for fall, with pumpkins and corn stalks adorning every light pole. Austin's office was not far from the law office and as we walked past I noticed there was a scarecrow perched outside the door, his arm raised in a perennial wave.

"You wanna go to Gene's?" he asked as we walked down the main street.

"Sure. I haven't been there since high school."

"So, how's it going so far? You miss the big city?"

I shook my head. "St. Louis never felt like home. It'll be an adjustment being back, though. I was working on a murder case at my old firm and the work's a little different here. Dad said the public defender needs some help, so I might do that part time."

I glanced at my watch as we walked into Gene's. It was a little after one, but the place was still packed. The savory scent of grilling burgers was just as I remembered it.

Austin found us a small two-person table by a window. I squeezed my big frame in, my long legs bumping into my brother's beneath the table. When I scanned the menu, I saw all the downhome food I'd been missing.

"Hi, what can I get you two to drink?" a waitress asked. I looked up and met blue eyes framed by dark auburn lashes. Her long hair of the same color was pulled back in a ponytail.

The word beautiful didn't do this woman justice. She was tall and lean. Fair, with pink lips and a smile I couldn't look away from. I was probably grinning like a dumbass, but with those sky-colored eyes on me, I couldn't bring myself to care.

"Reed." Austin kicked me under the table. "What do you want to drink?"

"Oh." I shook my head to clear it. "Water's good."

"Be right back with those." She turned and her ponytail swung, revealing the back of her neck. My gaze inadvertently traveled lower, to her perfect, toned ass.

"Jesus, put your tongue back in your mouth," Austin said.

I turned to him. "Sorry. I just . . . who is she? I was expecting Tammy or Margie."

Tammy was a fixture at Gene's. She was a waitress with no teeth and a large, hairy mole on one cheek. Though it was hard to understand what she was saying sometimes, she was one of the nicest people in Lovely.

"I think Tammy moved away a couple years ago," Austin said. "That's Ivy."

"She's gorgeous. I didn't mean to stare like that, but . . . wow."

Austin shrugged. "I think she's used to it."

"What's her story?"

"I don't know. She's worked here since right after I moved my office downtown, so . . . three years? I see her around town sometimes with Gene and Margie. She's a single mom. Has a little boy."

"Is she seeing anyone?"

Austin shook his head. "I know a couple guys who asked her out, but she says no every time."

We both quieted as she returned with our waters.

"What can I get you guys?" she asked.

"Ivy, this is my brother Reed. He just moved home to join our dad's practice."

She smiled my way. "Nice to meet you, Reed. Welcome home."

Damn, I loved the sound of her saying my name. I'd never had such a strong, immediate pull toward a woman.

"Thanks. If you, uh . . . need an attorney for anything, you know, I'm just down the block."

She arched a brow with amusement. "I try not to do anything that would require a legal defense."

"Oh, right . . . no, I didn't mean it like . . . I probably sound like an ambulance chaser right now. I do criminal defense, but I wasn't trying to insinuate you'll need one." I blew out a breath and grinned. "Sorry."

"Jesus, just order some lunch," Austin muttered.

"The special is meatloaf with a side of mashed potatoes," Ivy said. Her pen was poised over her notepad as she looked at me.

"Is the meatloaf any good?" I asked her.

She paused for a beat. "Uh . . . A lot of people seem to like it but, I have to say, you can't beat Gene's burgers."

"Got it. I'll take a cheeseburger and fries."

"Same," Austin said. "Thanks, Ivy."

She nodded and turned. I scrubbed a hand down my face to clear away the daze she'd left me in.

"Been a while, I take it?" Austin asked.

I shrugged. "Couple months. But I didn't make an ass of myself like that because I was hoping to hook up with her. It's just . . . she's just . . ."

"Yeah. But I don't think she dates. You gonna give Meredith a call?"

The mention of my ex-girlfriend's name made me grunt in distaste. We'd been minutes away from being married in front of half the town when she just never showed up. Turned out she'd met an older guy with a yacht and she decided to take a chance on him. I hadn't realized it at the time, but she'd done me a huge favor.

"No. We're over and I plan to keep it that way."

"Just for a casual thing, I meant. So you can stop

drooling over waitresses when you go out for lunch."

I shook my head adamantly. "I'm not interested in Meredith. I'm over her, anyway. I work late and go to the gym every night. I don't have time for women."

"Bet you'd make time for the right one."

I said nothing, my gaze following Ivy across the diner. She was quick and graceful, evading the guy who shoved his chair out without looking behind him, nearly hitting her. Her smile made everything else in the room look dull. An older man standing at the cash register said something to her and she laughed and gave his shoulder an affectionate squeeze. Lucky bastard.

Yeah. If she'd agree to a date with me, I'd definitely make time.

SIX

Ivy

LUNCH RUSH WOULD BE over soon. My tables all had their food and now I was just refilling drinks and bringing checks. Mondays were always crazy busy. Good thing I'd eaten some toast at the start of my shift this morning, because I hadn't had time for even a bite of lunch.

I delivered a tall vanilla milkshake to a toddler who smiled gleefully when she saw it. She looked around three years old, the same age as my Noah. As soon as I set the tall glass in front of her, she swiped the cherry from the top and stuck it in her mouth.

"Mmm," she said, grinning.

I glanced at the girl's well-dressed mother, who'd stacked sacks from the shopping they'd apparently done in an empty seat at their table. One of my dreams was to take Noah shopping for new clothes and shoes without having to worry about every dollar.

Fortunately he was young enough that he didn't

realize most everything he wore was secondhand. He'd be bursting with energy when I picked him up from daycare this afternoon. I got there right after his post-nap snack every day, and we usually headed home to play. It wasn't warm enough for the park anymore.

Austin and Reed Lockhart were in the cash register line, and I snuck a glance at Austin's brother. All the Lockhart boys were tall and handsome, but Reed was unique. He seemed taller than the others and he had broad shoulders—he looked as if he worked out a lot. One thing was for sure, he had a presence that couldn't be ignored.

I did a quick glance around all my tables. Lucy Mackin's Coke was a little under half full, so I headed for her table to grab it for a refill. I was passing by my young milkshake customer's table when I heard her wailing.

I'd swing by in a sec and see if some crackers or crayons would help. As I was passing the crying toddler one of my feet slid out from beneath me. All I could get out was a quick yelp before all the breath was sucked out of my lungs.

Crap. My arms flew out as I sought to grab something to break my fall but I was out of luck.

I prepared to hit the floor but was surprised when an arm wrapped around my back, stopping my fall. My hands were still scrambling for purchase, and one of them landed on a solid forearm.

"I've got you," a deep voice said. He pulled me halfway up and what little air I'd gotten back in my lungs left in a rush. Reed Lockhart was looking down at me, his dark brown eyes brimming with concern.

My heart was racing from the scare I'd just had, but being in Reed's arms wasn't going to slow it down. I was close enough to see his dark five-o-clock shadow and take in his faint, woodsy scent.

And those eyes. I couldn't look away. They were just a shade lighter than his dark brown hair. He was boyish and manly at the same time.

"You okay?" he asked. He still held me in a pose that looked like we were on Dancing With the Stars.

"Yes," I said breathlessly. "I'm fine. Thanks for saving me from wiping out. I didn't think anyone even saw me slip."

He eased me up slowly, leaving his warm, powerful arm around the small of my back.

"Instinct, I guess," he said, the corners of his lips quirking up a little.

"Well . . . thanks again."

He gave a half shrug and led me out of the vanilla milkshake puddle. "I'm just glad I was here. You sure you're okay?"

I held his gaze for another second before nodding. There was no reason for me to feel breathless anymore, but I did. When he slid his arm out from around me, I missed it immediately. No one but Noah had touched me in a long time. I liked it that way, but Reed's solid presence reminded me what was missing from my life.

Stepping back, I took a deep breath. That kind of closeness would always be missing. I'd closed off my heart to all men a long time ago. There would never be another man who would hurt or disappointed me, because no one was getting in. My life was about me and Noah, and we didn't need anyone else.

REED

I WAS STILL RATTLED on the walk back to my office. After Austin had gone in the direction of his own office I couldn't think of anything but Ivy. The way she'd felt in my arms, the rise and fall of her chest as I looked down at her and those bright blue eyes looking up at me.

She hadn't expected anyone to catch her. She'd been planning to land flat on her ass. I could tell that by the way she'd clutched my arm, her expression a mixture of surprise and gratitude. It made me want to pull her closer and tell her I'd catch her again if she needed me to. I'd catch her anytime she wanted.

I shook my head at the sentimental nonsense I was thinking. Maybe Austin was right and all the months of not getting laid were catching up with me.

"Hey, Lena," I said when I walked in the front door to the office. "Any messages?"

"No messages, but there's someone in your office," she said, not looking up from whatever she was writing.

I walked down the hall and into my office, which still smelled like the leather law books Dad had kept in here before I joined the practice. When I tossed my coat on a chair, a woman stood up from the wingback chair in the corner of the room.

"Reed," she said softly. "It's good to see you."

Meredith. My good mood took a nose dive.

"What are you doing here?"

"I moved back home a few months ago."

"No, I mean what are you doing here in my office?"

"I wanted to see you." It was obvious she was look-ing for a warmer reception than I was offering.

I shook my head with disgust. "Look, I've got work to do and, to be honest, you shouldn't have been let in here. You need to go."

"Are you still mad at me?" she continued. "It's been five years, Reed."

"I'm not mad, I'm busy."

She gave me the puppy dog eyes I'd fallen for back when we were together. "Can we have dinner soon? To catch up?"

"That's not a good idea, Meredith."

"We never talked about things."

"That was your choice, not mine. And it was years ago. There's no point in talking about it now—I've moved on."

She took a step closer to me and tried to lay a palm on my chest, but I stepped back and her hand met empty space.

"Reed," she said, laughing. "Are you afraid I'll seduce you with one touch?"

Aggravation flared in my veins. "No. I just don't want you touching me. I'm busy."

"Why are you treating me like a stranger?"

"Because you are one. The day you left me at the altar was the day I realized I really had no idea who you were."

"Well, now that we're both home again, maybe we can work on that. I've missed you."

"I'm not interested."

Meredith gave me a pleading look. "I'm divorced now, you know. That whole thing . . . it was such a huge mistake, Reed."

"Look—"

She stepped forward again, this time laying her hand

on my crotch rather than my chest.

"Surely you haven't forgotten this," she said in a low tone, rubbing my dick.

My breath came out in a shudder. The timing of Meredith's come on was really fucking bad. I was still fired up from having Ivy in my arms, so vulnerable and pretty. But I couldn't have her right now, and I sure as hell wouldn't let Meredith stand in.

I moved her hand away from my dick and she groaned sadly.

"Are you seeing someone? Is that it?"

"That's actually none of your business, but no. Just to be clear, there's no chance of us getting back together. Now I've got work to do, so . . ." I nodded at the open doorway.

She sighed deeply then gave me a dirty look and walked out. Once she was gone I called Lena into my office and let her know, in no uncertain terms, that I was not happy with her unprofessional behavior. Then, she too gave me a dirty look and left my office.

It wasn't that I had hard feelings toward Meredith; those had passed a long time ago. What we'd had between us was long gone. Now, having seen her again for the first time in five years, I sure as hell didn't feel the magic we'd had at first when we got together in high school. She'd been my first and I'd been hers. And then we'd settled into a steady, happy relationship. But that was all water under the bridge. I had absolutely zero interest in her.

Before moving home I'd decided that I wasn't getting into anything serious with any woman—I didn't need the grief. But already I was feeling an urge to go back to Gene's and ask Ivy out. I wanted to find out more about her. So far all I knew was that she was a beautiful single mom who'd bewitched me in a matter of minutes.

Meeting Ivy had been unplanned and unexpected but, yeah, it felt really damned good. Magic.

SEVEN

Ivy

LUNCH RUSH WAS OVER for the day, and I was wiping down the front counter and refilling salt and pepper shakers. Margie, who rarely stopped moving at work, was leaning against the counter and staring at the TV mounted from the ceiling. The TV was there for our customers who liked to watch the morning news while having their breakfasts. We kept the volume turned all the way down, but people liked to read the headlines at the bottom of the screen.

Margie had turned on the subtitles and was shaking her head with disapproval.

"If I met that guy on the street, I'd cut his balls off," she said simply, as though she was discussing the weather.

"Geez, Margie, he's just a guy on TV," I said, smiling.

"Look at this," she said, pointing up at the screen. I looked at it and rolled my eyes when I saw that she was watching Springer. The show's topic, 'I Married my Daddy,' was plastered onto the bottom of the screen. My stomach rolled with nausea as I looked at the people screaming at each other on the screen. A middle-aged man was passionately kissing a woman who didn't look more than twenty, while another man raised a chair up from the floor, preparing to launch it at the guy I presumed was 'Daddy' in this scenario.

"She's pregnant with his child," Margie said, sounding shocked. "That kid will probably be born deformed. Poor thing."

I tried to calm my racing heart, reminding myself that no one here knew my truth. My secret was so safe that I could judge the people on that TV screen along with Margie and no one would be the wiser. I wouldn't do it though. That young woman and her unborn baby didn't deserve derision from a stranger like me.

I lined up sugar packets in dishes on the counter, saying a silent prayer that the baby would be born healthy and the woman would come to her senses and begin a new life without the idiot who admitted to being her father and her lover.

"What kind of monster could get it up for his own child?" Margie said, her expression twisted with disgust. "It's sick. He belongs in prison."

The counter was clean and I was relieved for the opportunity to take my used towels back to the washing machine off the kitchen. This was why I kept my secret–because I couldn't stand the thought of me and Noah being judged. I'd considered telling Margie I had been sexually assaulted. I trusted her and, despite her hair trigger temper, she was a very good person. But I knew she'd press for details, and I wasn't ready to give them.

I lost myself in dishes and laundry until my shift was over. Then I stopped by the Lovely Public Library. The small red brick building was one of my favorite places in town. I checked books out by the dozen and used the computers for free Internet access when I needed it.

I was making a quick stop to use a computer today. The head librarian, Lillian, waved at me from the front desk to tell me it was okay to use a computer without signing in.

When I logged onto my email, I saw that I had a waiting message from April. We'd kept in close touch by email over the past three years. Seeing her name on the screen made me smile before I'd even opened the message. I clicked on it and sat back in my chair to read it.

Hello, Ivy. I miss you and wish you'd come to Seattle for a visit. It still doesn't quite feel like home. Thanks for the pictures of Noah. He's such a beautiful boy. I'll be mailing a box of Christmas gifts for you guys soon. Just remember that the saying about real friends not buying their friends' children drum sets is completely false.

Things were going well with me and Dave, but he interviewed for a job in Florida last week and it sounds like he's going to get it. He asked me to move there with him, but we've only been dating for three months. It's too soon. We're talking about a long distance relationship. Guess we'll see if it works out.

What about you? I hope you're still helping with the hospital foundation. One of these days some hot doctor will sweep you off your feet if you'll just let him. You can't live in a cocoon forever.

Even though I don't know the details, I know you've been hurt—badly. Just don't let that define you, Ivy. You're smart, caring and an amazing mother to Noah.

Speaking of you being smart, have you thought any more about starting college classes? I know you're busy, but you can take classes online from your local community college. I'll help with the application and financial aid process. You can do it, Ivy. The hardest part is getting started.

My prep period is almost over, so I better go. Oh, one more thing . . . I signed up for a 5K in the spring. Can you believe it? I may collapse halfway through, but that's what hot paramedics are for, right?

Much love,
April

Tears pricked my eyes as I read the message again. April meant the world to me and her messages always reminded me of our brief time as roommates. I glanced at my watch and saw that I had time to write a quick message back.

Dear April,

I miss you, too. Things here are good. Noah has a new fascination with trains. I'm thinking of taking him to ride one sometime. There is a small commuter train nearby so maybe I'll try that. One day, maybe we'll take the train to Seattle!

You'll be happy to know I applied online to the local community college and I got in. I think I'll take one class next semester. They said I'm also eligible for a scholarship, so that will really help.

Today I slipped and fell at work. It was really embarrassing. A customer caught me so it wasn't as bad as it could have been.

Sorry to hear about Dave moving. He sounds like a really great guy. Maybe the long distance thing will work out.

I'm so proud of you for signing up for the 5K! You'll be

amazing. Or . . . hot paramedic. Sounds like a win-win.
  Off to pick up Noah. Take care.
  xo Ivy

April had been encouraging me to try dating for more than a year now. Every time, I avoided the subject or I'd make vague promises about trying. She meant well, but she didn't understand my distrust of men . . . and how could she? I knew there was some truth to what she was saying, but I just wasn't ready for any of that right now.

I left the library and drove the five minutes over to Noah's daycare and went inside, smiling at the sounds of kids playing. When I got to Noah's room, he squealed and ran into my open arms. My heart swelled as he locked his arms around me in a hug.

"Hi, lovebug," I said. "Ready to go home?"

"Yeah!" he cried happily. He took my hand and led me to the wall where the picture he'd painted earlier was displayed, the paint still a little wet. It was a swirl of shades of red and blue.

"What is it?" I asked, looking down at him.

"A doggie," he said proudly.

"I love it."

We said goodbye to his teacher and left to head home for dinner. I buckled him into his car seat and the trip home was filled with his happy chatter.

"Christmas tree!" he cried gleefully when we passed an evergreen. He pointed out evergreens every time he saw one, no matter what season it was.

"That's a tall one," I said. "We'll be getting a Christmas tree in a couple months. What do you want for Christmas, Noah?"

"Pancakes."

I laughed and glanced at him in the rearview mirror while my car idled at a stoplight. His light brown hair had a hint of curl and he shared my blue eyes. He was my whole world in one adorable little package.

"Do you want some new racecars?" I asked.

"Yeah. And pancakes."

"I bet Gene will make us some pancakes on Christmas morning. He knows how much you love them."

We'd spent the past two Christmases with Gene and Margie. They were crazy about Noah. We also spent Friday nights with them, usually playing cards and making homemade pizza. After Noah had fallen asleep there a couple times, Margie had insisted that we stay in their guest room on Friday nights.

The next couple of hours passed by in a blur. By the time I'd played trains with Noah, made dinner, washed the dishes and given him a bath, I barely had the energy to get a shower and climb into bed. I read for less than five minutes before I turned out the light. Our mornings always started early—well before sunrise—and I needed all the sleep I could get.

The next day I dropped Noah off at daycare and went into work. We were short a morning waitress, which meant me and Margie had to work harder than usual.

I knew most of my customers well. Most were farmers meeting for coffee and gossip, or retired people who came in for some company. Time flew as I poured, served and chatted. I'd stopped for a quick drink of water when Margie approached and gave me a look.

"Walter's getting impatient," she said in a tone only I could hear. I glanced down the front counter to the stool on the end, where a man with sparse gray hair was scowling at me.

"On it," I said.

"Oh, here comes Ben Henderson," Margie added in the same hushed tone. "He left his wife for their *babysitter* over the weekend. Can you *believe* that? I used to respect him, too. Poor Dena's just mortified. And how do you think their poor kids must feel?"

I'd learned Margie didn't care if I responded to her gossip as long as she thought I was listening. I nodded in acknowledgement and then walked down to greet Walter.

"Good morning, sir. What'll it be?"

"Should I order breakfast, or is it lunch time now?" He tapped his wristwatch and squinted his eyes at it.

"It's seven forty, so I think you're still good for breakfast."

"Hmph." He opened the menu and scanned it. I played along, though we both knew exactly what he would order. He'd been coming in every weekday for several months, and he always ordered the same thing.

"Two eggs, over medium. Wheat toast with real butter. Small dish of plain oatmeal," he finally said. "And black coffee."

"Got it." I scrawled his order in my pad and took his menu. "And I'm sorry I kept you waiting, Walter."

"I'd rather wait for you than have one of the other servers," he said, looking at me over the wire rims of his glasses. "There's you or that fellow with greasy hair and open facial sores."

"Don just busses tables. And there's Margie, too."

He grunted his distaste. "Too chatty."

"I think what you're trying to say is that you like me. And I like you, too."

"My dear, no one *likes* me. And I don't much like anyone either. I make an excellent recluse."

"I started reading one of your books the other night."

"Oh?"

I nodded. "It's good. It moved a little slow in the beginning, but now I'm into it."

Walter grinned with amusement. "Which one is it?"

"Lucky Seven."

He waved a hand. "Only made the *New York Times* sixteen weeks in a row. You're right to be unimpressed."

"I didn't say I'm not impressed. You're a famous author. That's quite impressive in itself."

"Bah."

I winked and headed for the pass through to the kitchen to deliver his order. Margie had told me when Walter first came in that he was actually Tom Hobson, the famous suspense novelist. I knew his pen name—everyone did—but behind it was Walter Grieves, a slightly grouchy man who liked his privacy. He'd moved to Lovely several years ago seeking anonymity, which was probably why I'd bonded with him immediately.

He'd been a morning regular at the Lovely Café until he was permanently ejected for yelling at a waitress over his burnt toast. And now he was a regular at Gene's.

He tipped me precisely fifteen percent every day and always let me know when his coffee wasn't just right. I'd grown attached to seeing him every day. It thrilled me to think I got to have conversations with a man who went home after breakfast to pen another bestseller. Lovely was small and imperfect, but it was my home now. It gave me a measure of pride to know someone rich and successful would chose Lovely as his home above all other places.

I wasn't rich or successful, but I was grateful for the friendships of Margie and Gene . . . and Walter. Every day I was glad the blue butterfly had led me to Lovely.

REED

FOR THE FIRST TIME since moving home, I was able to hang out with the three of my brothers who lived here. Kyle had the afternoon off, but was on call at the hospital. Austin was always off on Sundays, and Mason set his own hours since he ran his own tech business.

We were playing two on two at the gym, a place we'd spent thousands of hours at when we were growing up. I'd missed playing with my brothers, because we shared the same competitive nature.

The only sounds on the court were the bouncing ball, our shoes squeaking against the polished surface and the occasional grunt or swear word. I was sweating heavily from the best workout I'd had since getting home.

"How's it going with Dad?" Kyle asked me during a quick break. "He giving you all the shit work?"

"Not yet."

"How's the dog doing?"

"Snoop's good. We go for a run every morning at the dog park. He comes to the office with me some days."

"The boys have been asking to come see him," Kyle said, a hint of regret in his expression.

Snoop had become my dog after Kyle bought him as a surprise for his two sons. After two days his wife Kim declared that she was taking him to the shelter because he stank like dog and got hair on her new couch. When Kyle called me and begged me to take the dog, I could hear the boys crying in the background. I'd driven to Lovely that evening to get him.

"Bring them over," I said. "They can stay the night

with me and visit with Snoop all they want. I'll take them to the dog park with us."

"They'd like that," Kyle said. "Maybe next weekend."

We started back at the game and Mason sank a three pointer and then turned to me.

"You going to the hospital foundation fundraiser Friday night?"

"Yeah, Mom roped me in."

"It's a good time, man," he said. "Last year I had some kickass moonshine that Tubby Taylor made."

"I'm selling raffle tickets—which reminds me, you guys better be good for at least fifty bucks each worth of tickets."

"Oh, yeah?" Austin yelled as he ran down the court. "What are you gonna do if we don't—sue us?"

We all laughed and then I said, "I'm just glad I don't have to wear a tux or anything dressy. Mom said jeans would be just fine."

"Yeah, she's right. It'll be held in MacArthur's barn again this year," Kyle said. "Everyone will be wearing jeans and boots."

We all walked over to the bench for a break. I wiped the sweat from my face with a towel and sat down to stretch my legs.

"When are we gonna get back to boxing?" I asked Kyle, my best opponent in the ring.

My oldest brother shook his head and gave me an apologetic look. "No more boxing for me. I sprained a finger last time and it fucked up my surgery schedule."

"No shit? I guess surgeons do have to watch out for their hands. Well damn, who am I gonna box with now?"

"Me," Mason said.

I laughed until I realized he was serious. "I'd clean

your clock and you'd be pissed off for the next two years," I said.

"I would not."

"You fight like a girl."

"Suck my cock." He shoved me and I couldn't help laughing again.

"Alright, I'll spar with you," I said. "Just don't cry about it when I bruise up your pretty face."

He shrugged. "I'm not worried. *If* that happens I'll tell everyone I stopped a robbery or something, and it'd probably get me laid."

"Whatever I can do to help the cause," I said sarcastically. Mason was a confirmed bachelor with no desire to have a serious girlfriend.

"Let's do it. After the hospital fundraiser thing. Mom would have our asses if we showed up to that with black eyes."

"Hell, yeah, she would."

I hadn't been back in Lovely for long, but already I couldn't imagine leaving the place again. My dream was to start a legal aid nonprofit, and my hometown was the perfect place to do it. Hopefully in time I'd be known as something other than the guy who got ditched at the altar.

EIGHT

Ivy

I STOOD AT THE entrance to the most enormous old barn I'd ever seen. Laughter and music drifted out from the red two-story structure. Two huge doors were propped open, beckoning me to join the party.

What was I doing here? I actually knew the answer to that question. I'd been asked to help sell raffle tickets at this barn dance by Grace Lockhart and I just couldn't say no. When she'd told me it was for the Lovely Hospital Foundation, and that no dancing would be required, I'd been all too happy to help out.

But social situations involving me and makeup made me nervous. I was woefully out of practice. Usually, on Friday nights, I had my hair up in a ponytail and was making pizza with Noah, Margie and Gene. Instead, they were making pizza without me this time. But I still planned to go to their house for the night when I was done. Noah loved our weekly sleepover at Margie and

Gene's.

Maybe tonight wouldn't be so bad. I adored Grace, and the hospital foundation was a cause close to my heart. Fortunately this event was casual. I was wearing my favorite old dark jeans, a green blouse I'd scored for a dollar at a garage sale and brown ballet flats. Hopefully I was rustic enough for a barn dance.

When I walked in, I couldn't help breaking out in a big smile. The inside of the barn had been transformed. Lights were strung from the rafters and the walls were decorated with wreaths of fresh flowers. The lively music I'd heard was from a group with fiddles and other string instruments. Couples were already spinning around on the wood dance floor.

"Ivy, you made it!" Grace approached and embraced me warmly. Her dark shoulder length hair was held back with a headband in a red handkerchief pattern. Like me, she wore jeans and a simple blouse.

"Hi, Grace," I said. "Thanks for asking me to come."

"You look so pretty, as always."

"Well, I came to work, so you just let me know what you need."

"I've got you at the raffle and 50/50 ticket table. Right over here."

She led the way to a long folding table and I did a double take when I saw who was sitting there. Reed rose to greet me, smiling sheepishly.

"Hey, Ivy," he said. "Nice to see you again."

He wore jeans and a blue flannel shirt, his five o'clock shadow a little more grown out this time. And damn, was he *tall*. Reed looked more at home in his casual clothes than he had in his dark, perfectly tailored suit. And, surprisingly, he looked even more handsome this way.

I laughed nervously. "You, too. I promise I won't slip on any milkshakes tonight."

"I'm a little disappointed to hear that."

My heart had turned into an out of control drum, pounding to no particular rhythm. The way he was looking at me, his brown eyes so warm and . . . interested. Not just attracted but *interested* . . . it was unnerving.

"Oh," Grace said, looking back and forth between us. "So you two have already met?"

"Yeah, Reed and Austin came into Gene's the other day and he saved me from wiping out on a wet patch on the floor," I said.

"Well, I should hope so. I'm proud to say I raised five gentlemen." Then, changing the subject she added, "Reed already knows all the details on the tickets sales. Have a seat, Ivy." She gestured at the folding chair next to Reed's. "I'll send in a replacement later so you can enjoy the dance."

"Oh, I'm just here to work," I said. "Don't worry about relief for me."

Grace nodded and smiled before heading away. I went around to the other side of the table and set my purse down beneath it. Reed was still standing. I was about to ask him if everything was okay when he pulled out my chair for me.

"Thanks," I said, sitting down. He slid the chair back in and then took his seat again.

Ticket sales were brisk and we sold tickets for a while, mostly chatting with the people buying them. Everyone knew Reed. I tried not to eavesdrop, but a conversation between him and an older woman caught my attention.

"Reed, I'm so glad you came home, honey. You shouldn't be ashamed to show your face in Lovely."

"Thanks, Mrs. DeGeorge. No shame here. I was working in St. Louis after law school."

The white-haired woman gave him a skeptical look through her thick-rimmed glasses. "But you got stood up at your own wedding. That's humiliating. It's okay to admit it."

I heard Reed sigh softly. "It was five years ago. I've definitely moved on. And it's great to see you, Mrs. DeGeorge. How many raffle tickets would you like?"

"Just one, dear. And as long as we're talking . . . well, you know I was one of the guests at the wedding that day. I sent a nice blender as a gift, because your mother was so good to me after my Don died. And, well, since you didn't actually get married . . . I'd like the blender back."

There was a moment of silence. I forced my expression to stay neutral, though it was hard to not even crack a smile.

"I'm sorry to hear about that, Mrs. Degeorge," Reed said. "I don't know where the blender is, but I can pay you back so you can buy a new one."

"Oh, that's good of you. It seems like it was forty-seven dollars if I remember right."

She looked at him expectantly and he pulled his wallet from his back pocket and counted out some bills.

"I don't have change so we'll just make it an even fifty," he said.

"You're such a dear," Mrs. DeGeorge said, handing back one of the bills to pay for her raffle ticket. "Save a dance for me tonight. I'm not spoken for anymore, you know."

Reed handed over her change and gave her a polite smile. I made sure Mrs. DeGeorge was out of earshot before I laughed softly.

"Subtlety is a lost art in Lovely," I said, giving him a sympathetic look.

"Ain't that the truth," he muttered. "It wasn't the end of the world. I was supposed to get married five years ago. I've been over it since then, but sometimes it seems like no one except me wants to forget about it."

"So, she just didn't show up? That's pretty harsh."

"Yeah." He shrugged. "Just wasn't meant to be, so it was best to find out before the wedding, even though I wish it had happened differently."

"Very true. And did you, uh . . . ever meet someone else?"

He looked over and gave me a small smile. "No, I'm still a bachelor. How 'bout you? I hear you've shot down most every single guy in Lovely."

My cheeks warmed. "Definitely not that many. I have a little boy. If I'm not working, I'm with him. I don't have time for a social life right now."

"What's his name?"

"Noah. He's three. He's actually . . . the reason I came tonight. When I came to Lovely, I was pregnant and alone. I didn't have health insurance. The hospital foundation covered all the costs of my delivery. I would have been in debt for the rest of my life without that gift. Now I help raise money for the foundation to give back."

Reed nodded knowingly. "That's how you got to know my mom, then. She's always been active with the foundation."

"Yes. She taught me to knit and she's the reason Margie and I bake fifty pies for the bake sale every year."

"I'm gonna need to know when that is. I've got a weakness for apple pie." His serious look turned into a grin. "So Noah must keep you busy."

"He does."

"Does he like sports?"

I laughed and furrowed my brow. "He's only three."

"Yeah, but that's old enough to chase a ball around. Bring him by the gym sometime if you want and I'll lower one of the hoops and teach him some basketball."

"You play basketball?"

"Ever since I started walking."

"I guess it makes sense since you're so tall. How tall are you, exactly?"

"Six-four."

"Wow."

"Seriously, if you ever want an afternoon to yourself some weekend, I'll play basketball with Noah. He's probably too young for boxing."

"Are you kidding?"

He gave me a lopsided grin. "Yeah, I'm kidding. I'd never box with a kid."

"I'd take kickboxing at the gym if I had time."

"Yeah? I could teach you how to box if you want. You could hit me, but I wouldn't hit back."

"I've wanted to learn some kind of self-defense for a while."

"I can help with boxing, or teaching you how to shoot."

My eyes widened with surprise. "With a gun?"

"Yeah." He laughed. "I'm a hunter, but I'm decent with handguns too."

"Really? That's good, I guess."

Reed grinned and nudged my shoulder with his arm. "Quit looking at me like I'm a serial killer. This is the Bible belt. Guns are an everyday thing here."

"I know. But they're not my thing."

His gaze was warm. "So what is your thing?"

"I don't really have any *things*. I'm always working, or I'm with Noah. I read sometimes when he goes to sleep. And I was on the dance team in high school, but that was so long ago."

"How long?"

"You're asking how old I am?"

"In a roundabout way, yep."

"I'm 22."

Grace approached the table, her cheeks flushed. I'd seen her running around all evening to coordinate things.

"I'm closing up ticket sales since the drawings are coming up in about five minutes," she said. "You two go enjoy yourselves. There's plenty of food if you're hungry."

"Actually, I'm hoping for a dance," Reed said. He stood and held a hand out to me.

I pushed back a wave of nervous excitement. "Oh, I don't—"

"Dance?" His lopsided grin was back. "Tell me another one. I'm sure you haven't forgotten how in four years, Ivy. Come on."

"Go on," Grace said. "Have some fun, Ivy."

"I don't . . ." I paused, unable to finish the sentence. My mind was racing and what I wanted to say was that I didn't touch men, but I knew that would sound weird.

And it *was* weird, but it was true. Other than customers bumping into me at work, I hadn't touched a man since that awful night in my bedroom four year ago.

But Reed looked expectant and sincere. I wanted to say yes, but I stayed seated in my chair.

"C'mon. Save me from Mrs. DeGeorge," he said in a teasing tone.

I laughed and took a deep breath before sliding my hand into his. His hand was much bigger than mine, and the warmth of his touch made my heart race.

Reed led me onto the wooden dance floor and I avoided the gazes directed toward us. I could practically hear the Lovely rumor mill churning to life. It was just a dance, but in Lovely it would be grounds for morning coffee shop conversation.

When Reed turned and put a hand on my lower back, I sucked in a nervous breath. He was a good dancer, and he led me around the floor slowly so I could get the hang of it.

The sweet smell of hay lingered in the barn. People nearby were laughing and talking happily. I tried to focus on what was happening around us, but it was hard to think about anything but the warm brown eyes on me.

His sweet, disarming small talk had put me at ease when we were selling tickets, but now he said nothing, and my heart was once again racing uncontrollably. He just held me close and led me in time to the music. When the song switched, neither of us made a move to stop dancing.

I didn't want to like dancing with Reed. My past had made me strong and absolutely certain there was nothing I couldn't handle. I didn't need anyone but Noah. And I didn't need this closeness with Reed, but I admitted to myself that I liked it.

My hand rested on Reed's broad, firm shoulder. His warm gaze made me feel something I'd never experienced. I felt womanly, and maybe even a little alluring. It was a delicious thrill.

This was so different from dancing with Levi at junior prom. He'd groped my ass, kissed my neck and pressed his erection against me. Reed was a gentleman, and I was more aroused by the look in his eyes than I ever was by anything Levi did or said to me.

When the music ended an announcer said it was time for the drawings. Reed led me off the dance floor by the hand. He made his way through the crowd with me in tow, stopping at a table with food and drinks.

"You want some cider?" he asked. I nodded and he ladled me a cup. It was warm and spicy, and I didn't think until I'd finished half of it to ask if it was spiked with alcohol.

"Nah, I think it was made by the ladies from the church league," Reed said. "But I bet we can find some moonshine if you're wanting something stronger."

I shook my head and sipped the cider. "Just this is perfect for me."

We were making our way to a table to sit down when a group of men approached and one of them put an arm around Reed. They were all tall and dark and I recognized one of them as his brother Austin. These had to be the rest of the Lockhart boys. All but one of them, anyway.

"Hey man, how's it going?" one of them said to Reed.

"Ivy, these are my older brothers," Reed said. "Kyle, Mason and you already know Austin."

"I've seen you in the diner before," Mason said, reaching out to shake my hand. "Nice to meet you."

"You, too. There's one more brother, right?"

"Justin's at law school in Boston," Reed said. "He's the baby of the family."

A pretty blonde woman with big breasts too firm to be real came up and slid in beside Kyle.

"My sister-in-law Kim," Reed said. "Kim, this is Ivy."

"Hey," Kim said, offering a quick smile. She looked

up at Kyle. "How long do we have to stay? I'd like to get dinner soon."

"There's food here," Mason suggested, pointing to the table nearby.

Kim scrunched her face with disgust. "Pigs in a blanket, or a pulled pork sandwich eaten at a folding table in a barn is *not* dinner, Mason."

"It is for me," Mason said, shrugging. "Those corn muffin things are really good."

"You feel like walking outside?" Reed asked me in a low tone.

"Actually, I should go. My work is done, so I'd better get home."

"Excuse us, guys," Reed said, putting a hand on my back and leading me away from the group. When we were alone, I looked up at him awkwardly.

"Thanks for the dance," I said. "Or . . . dances. Anyway, thanks. It was fun."

"Yeah, it was. I should be the one thanking you. I'll walk you to your car."

"You don't have to do that." I shook my head, my heart starting its wild pounding again. Would he try to kiss me? I didn't want that. I already felt an energy between us, and that would just confirm it.

I hadn't come to Lovely to find a man. I'd come to raise one, and dating was a distraction I didn't need.

"I want to," he said. "Do you have stuff you need to grab?"

"Just my purse. I left it under the table."

I got my purse and said goodnight to Grace. Reed walked me the short distance to my car, which was parked in the grass outside the barn.

"Is Noah at home with a babysitter?" he asked.

"He's with Margie and Gene. We spend Friday nights with them."

"Gene's a great guy. He's an old friend of my dad's."

Suddenly I was standing next to my old Toyota, and I dug my keys out of my purse. When I looked up at Reed, a moment of silence passed between us. The barn was filled with light and laughter, but we stood alone in the darkness. It was a perfectly orchestrated moment for a kiss.

Reed leaned down and pulled on my door handle, opening it for me.

"Goodnight, Ivy," he said, taking my hand for just a second and rubbing his thumb over my knuckles.

"Goodnight."

I slid into the driver's seat and he closed the door for me. I spent the drive to Margie and Gene's house replaying the evening in my head. The dancing, the conversation and the memories of Reed's warm brown gaze made me smile. It was best he hadn't kissed me. I knew that in my head, but my heart wasn't convinced. I pushed back the disappointment I felt, because it was weak and romantic, and deep down, I was neither of those things.

NINE

REED

MY LEGS WERE SCRUNCHED up in the back seat of Dad's pickup truck, and the smell of fish guts had taken over the entire cab. But after my first day of ice fishing in a decade, and a successful day at that, I couldn't complain.

"Did you get truck envy, Dad?" Austin asked from the front seat. "This thing's a monster. Looks like you'd need a CDL to drive it."

Dad laughed from the driver's seat. "I've waffled about getting a new one for a couple of years. I needed a bigger bed to hold all the hunting gear. And your mother likes this one better because it's more comfortable."

"You thawed out yet?" Mason asked me from the other side of the truck's back seat.

"I'm alright. Just starving."

"We can make some sandwiches when we get home," Dad said. "Or there's leftover beef stew from last night."

We rode in silence for the last couple of miles and when we arrived at mom and dad's place we all helped unload the gear and our haul of fish.

"Better go in through the sunroom and get our dirty boots off there," Dad said. I followed him around to the back door of the huge, renovated old house we'd grown up in.

I was surprised to see the room was filled with women who were knitting. The couch, loveseat and chairs were all full, and more chairs had been brought in. All of them had stilled their knitting needles to see what the cat was dragging in.

"Sorry to interrupt, ladies," Dad said. "I forgot it was knitting club day."

"Did you boys have any luck?" Mom asked.

"We did. Caught around a dozen."

I pulled off my stocking hat and kicked off my muddy boots on the tile floor. When I looked up, my eyes locked with Ivy's. She was sitting in a chair on the other side of the room. I couldn't help smiling. It'd been a week since the barn dance and I'd gone to Gene's for lunch every day since. I always got a little small talk from her, but she was so busy that it was never enough.

The pale pink baby blanket she was knitting was resting in her lap. Something inside me softened at the sight of her with a baby blanket.

Austin's wife Hannah was sitting near Ivy, and Austin walked over, bent down and kissed her. I felt a strong urge to greet Ivy the same way. I'd considered kissing her after the barn dance, but it didn't seem right since we hadn't even been on a date.

I couldn't be forward with Ivy, no matter how much I wanted to. Her eyes seemed to send me mixed signals: *I like you, but stay away from me.*

"Where's Alana?" Austin asked Hannah.

"Upstairs playing with the other kids and Donna. It's her turn to get worn out by them."

"We'll go play with 'em after we eat," Austin said, looking at me.

I nodded and stepped out of my coveralls.

"You feel free to just keep taking stuff off," a middle-aged woman next to me said in a low voice. "I won't complain."

"Mom doesn't let me do strip teases in the house," I said, winking. "She's still the boss."

I picked up my discarded coat and coveralls from the floor and headed for the kitchen, looking at Ivy again on the way. Our eyes locked before I had to turn away to avoid running into the door jamb. Damn, I wanted to see her again, and not at the diner. I wanted something more, though it wasn't a good idea. She wasn't a woman I wanted to play around with and based on my track record of a failed serious relationship, that probably wouldn't work, either.

"You gonna ask her out or what?" Austin asked, turning from his scan of the refrigerator's contents to look at me.

I gave him a look that shut him up. He unloaded lunch meat and cheese onto the big kitchen island.

"Hey, can you make me a sandwich, too?" I said.

"I'm not your servant," he muttered.

"You've got the stuff out already. I'm going to the bathroom. C'mon, just make me a sandwich."

"Fine."

"Make me one, too," Mason said from the kitchen table. "I want mine toasted and cut in half."

"And I want a folded up note on my plate about how much you love me," I said, smirking.

I missed his grumbled response on my way to the bathroom. But by the time I got back to the kitchen, he was the one looking smug.

"What's with the shit-eating grin?" I asked, taking the plate he offered.

"Oh, nothing. But Ivy did come in here just now to get a drink of water. She asked where the big sexy lumberjack went and I told her you were in the shitter."

"Shut the fuck up."

"I'm not lying about her coming in here. I think she was looking for you, but she didn't say anything."

I glanced at the door to the sunroom while I took a bite of my sandwich. I'd slept with quite a few women in St. Louis, but the thought of Ivy looking for me excited me more than any of them had.

Footsteps pounded down the stairs and then back up again, accompanied by laughing kids.

"We've been up since four and now we're gonna go get treated like human punching bags," Austin said, shaking his head.

"I'll catch up on sleep tonight."

"Yeah, must be nice. I'll be lucky if Alana sleeps past seven in the morning."

"Suck it up. Let's go play."

The dozen or so kids were mostly thrilled to see us, but a couple were scared. I was an enormous guy with a dark scruff-covered face. It probably was a little scary.

"Noah, it's okay," Donna said to one little boy.

"Noah? Is that Ivy's son?" I asked her.

"Yeah. Come on out, Noah."

A little boy with wavy light brown hair peeked out from behind her back. His wide blue eyes were a carbon copy of his mother's.

"Hey, Noah," I said, sitting down on the ground. "I'm Reed."

"He's scared of men," Donna said. "It's not you."

"It's okay. I'm just gonna play with this train."

My parents had converted an upstairs bedroom into a toy room for their grandchildren. I'd almost finished building a block tower on the train table for the train to drive under when Noah approached me cautiously.

"Choo choo train," he said, pointing at it and looking at me.

"Yeah, buddy. Let's drive it."

It took about the same amount of time for him to steal my heart that it had for his mom to. Either I'd suddenly gone soft, or fate was trying to tell me something.

Ivy

MY HEARTBEAT HAD FINALLY returned to a normal pace. It had skyrocketed when Reed walked in the door. I'd never looked twice at hunters who came into the diner dressed in camo but, on Reed, the rugged look was very sexy.

My mouth had watered at the sight of him stepping out of his camo coveralls and dropping them on the floor next to his brown canvas coat. His dark hair had been sticking up from when he'd pulled off his stocking cap and I wanted to fix it. Or maybe I just wanted to run my fingers through it.

When he looked at me, I got warm all over. No man had ever had that effect on me. I'd gone into the kitchen for a drink hoping to run into him.

I didn't date, but the way Reed made me feel gave me hope. Maybe I wasn't emotionally ruined after all. Maybe someday, when Noah was grown, I'd want to date again. I doubted it, but having hope was nice.

It was my laundry day, so as soon as knitting club was over, I went upstairs to get Noah. The sound of happy laughter coming from Henry and Grace's play room made me smile. Noah loved playing with other kids.

But when I opened the door, it wasn't a kid, but Reed who was making Noah laugh. My throat tightened at the sight of Noah on Reed's shoulders, brushing his fingers against the ceiling.

My son had never been close to any man but Gene, who was like a grandpa to him. Gene liked to do puzzles and color with Noah. Rambunctious boy play was something Noah didn't get outside of daycare.

I just watched, enjoying the moment. Seeing my little boy happy was the best feeling in the world. Reed turned and saw me. He smiled sheepishly and lifted Noah off his shoulders and put him back down on the floor.

"I want to touch the ceiling!" Noah cried, reaching his arms out to Reed.

"We have to go, sweetie," I said, approaching him and getting down on my knees. "We have to do laundry today."

His face fell.

"How about a scoop of ice cream tonight?" I said. "With chocolate syrup?"

"And spinkles." His mispronunciation of the word always melted me.

"And spinkles," I agreed.

"How was your knitting?" Reed asked me.

"It was good. Thanks for playing with Noah."

"It was fun. He's a really sweet kid, Ivy. You've done a great job."

His compliment touched me deeply. Being Noah's mom was more important to me than anything else.

"Thank you." I took Noah's hand. "Can you say bye, Noah?"

"Bye," Noah said so softly it was barely audible.

"Bye, Noah," Reed said. "Let's play trains again soon."

I met Reed's dark brown eyes one more time before turning to leave the room with Noah. There was an awkward tension of unspoken words between me and Reed. I was out of my element. Noah had warmed up to Reed, but I just couldn't allow myself to do that.

REED

I RUBBED MY EYES and put my reading glasses down. The stack of files on my desk was half the size it had been this morning. It was after six pm, and I had to get the hell out of here and get a workout in before the gym closed. I'd been in front of my desk doing research and billing all day.

I was wrapping up my last file for the night when a knocking sound from the front of the office caught my attention. I was the only one left here and the office was closed. Who the hell would knock after hours?

Maybe Lena was locked out. I got up to go see who was at the front door. I was surprised, and not in a good way, when I saw Meredith peeking at me through the glass.

"We're closed," I said as soon as I opened the door.

"I know. I just . . . I thought I saw your office light on, so I stopped. If you haven't eaten, can we have dinner at Jimmy's?"

I started to say no but she stopped me.

"I only want to talk. If I was trying to get with you, I'd be trying to get into your office right now. If you'll just hear me out . . . I just think we both need some closure. I know I do."

I rubbed my unshaven jaw line. I *was* hungry. But I sure as hell didn't want Meredith getting the wrong idea.

"Alright," I muttered. "We eat and you get closure and that's it. If you bring up us getting back together, I'm leaving."

She nodded and I went back in to get my coat. When I returned she was standing on the curb with her arms wrapped around herself. The bitter November temperatures weren't letting up.

"Are we walking or meeting there?" I asked.

"Might as well walk, it's not far."

We walked the block to Jimmy's Italian Place in silence. Despite the lackluster name, Jimmy's had great pizza and spaghetti. A greeter led us to a booth and I loosened my tie before sliding in.

The place was full. I was checking out the new red, green and white stripes on the wall when my gaze stopped on Ivy. She was at a booth across from us, and Noah sat on the other side.

He was laughing about something she'd said, and her face glowed as she smiled at him. I'd never seen this smile from her. It was one of open love and adoration. I wanted to be sitting in that booth with them.

"Reed," Meredith said, clearing her throat. "Ready to

order?"

The waitress was looking at me expectantly. I ordered a pizza and a soda and forced myself to look at Meredith instead of Ivy and Noah.

"How was work today?" she asked.

"Good."

"I'm working at my dad's car dealership doing book-keeping. I thought I'd hate it there, but it's not so bad."

I nodded, not caring if she took my lack of interest as rudeness. A few more seconds elapsed before she cleared her throat again.

"So . . . when I came to your office the other day, I was . . ." She sighed and gave me a sheepish look. "I was hoping you still had feelings for me."

"Meredith, I'm not—"

"Just let me finish, okay? I was hoping, but I wasn't surprised to find out there's nothing there for you any-more. It's been a really long time. I didn't appreciate what I had with you, and I regret it."

I leaned my elbows on the table and considered what she'd said, trying to come up with the right thing to say in response. Everything seemed like it would make her think I was open to getting back together, so I stayed qui-et.

"I'm sorry, Reed," she said softly. "I'm not saying that because I think you'll give me another chance. I'm truly sorry for not showing up that day. It was an awful thing to do and you didn't deserve it."

I shrugged nonchalantly. "In the scheme of things, it wasn't a big deal, Meredith. I'm completely over it and you should be, too."

I snuck a glance at Ivy and Noah. They were coloring a paper placemat together, both of them smiling happily.

"Do you want to know why?" Meredith asked.

Reluctantly, I met her gaze across the table. "Why what?"

"Why I didn't show up that day."

"We weren't right together. That's why enough for me."

"We were, though." She looked down at the red plastic tablecloth. "It wasn't that I didn't want you. I always did. I just caved under the pressure of your last name. Everyone in town is interested in the Lockharts. You're all attractive and successful and so damn nice. You guys coach and volunteer and run for the school board. I felt really young to be part of all that. I just wanted to travel and have fun . . . with you, but I knew you wouldn't want to leave your family."

"No, I wouldn't have. We wanted different things in life, and that's okay."

Meredith shook her head, her expression sad. "I was young and stupid. I ended up with a man who wanted what I thought I did, and it wasn't all that."

"You're still young. Don't give up on finding what you want."

"Just not with you," she said, her tone a mix of sarcasm and amusement.

"Right."

"You've got it bad for the waitress, don't you?"

"Her name's Ivy."

"And you can't stop looking at her. I saw you guys dancing at the barn dance. So are you guys a thing?"

"No."

"Why not? You like her and I think she likes you, too."

I sighed deeply. "I'm not talking about this with you."

"I hope she'll be smarter than I was."

"We're not dating. She doesn't date. Don't start any rumors, Meredith. It wouldn't be fair to her."

"Alright, alright." She put her hands up in surrender. "Let's go back to you staring at her and me pretending not to notice."

I cracked a smile. "I specifically planned to not settle down when I came back home. I'm here to work, and I keep so busy with everything that it's not really fair to the other person for me to be in a relationship."

"But now you're reconsidering because you like her so much."

I just looked at her, unwilling to admit or deny it.

"Life's too short not to go for it," she said. "Did I ruin you on commitment? Please tell me I didn't."

"I haven't had a committed relationship since you."

She sighed deeply. "Well, that makes me feel like shit. Most women would give anything for a guy like you, Reed."

"Yeah, I don't know." I rubbed the back of my neck restlessly.

Meredith gave me an intent look. "It wasn't you. It was me being young and stupid and it's my greatest regret. I don't know Ivy very well, but she seems like a woman who needs someone like you in her life."

"What do you mean?"

"She's super protective of her son. She's very private. Never goes out, never dates. The signs are all there."

I furrowed my brow. "What signs?"

"She's been hurt really bad."

I sat back against the booth, feeling like I'd had the wind knocked out of me. It made sense. The way she'd reacted when I caught her at the diner, her body tense and afraid. The way her eyes gave me two conflicting messages.

"I can't stand the idea of someone hurting her," I said. "It makes me sick. And really fucking angry."

"What does that tell you? You already feel protective of her. Be man enough to take a chance."

I looked at Meredith, seeing the woman I'd known so many years ago. "I would, but she doesn't date."

"So change her mind."

I looked over at Ivy and Noah. A plate of spaghetti sat on the table between them. She was cutting it up. When she blew on the first bite before holding the fork out to Noah, my pride became irrelevant. If any man was going to break through her walls and get in, it was damn well gonna be me.

TEN

Ivy

NOAH TOSSED THE SPOON aside and put his hands on the pizza crusts, spreading out the tomato sauce. It squished between his fingers and he smiled gleefully.

"There you go," Gene said. "Doin' it the old-fashioned way."

We were in Margie and Gene's kitchen, and I was more than ready for this Friday pizza night. It had been a busy week at the diner and, today, I'd only had time to eat half a grilled cheese. For some reason, the diner had been super busy all week.

"Remind me to bring a casserole over for the Tomlins tomorrow," Margie said to no one in particular as she set the table. "Tanya had a hysterectomy today."

"Time to sprinkle on the cheese," Gene said to Noah.

"Do you know she had a period that lasted more than a month?" Margie continued, turning to me, her brows arched.

"Hmm?" I looked up from the newspaper I'd been scanning. I'd only been half listening to Margie.

"Tanya Tomlin," Margie repeated. "That's one of the reasons she's getting a hysterectomy. And some sort of vaginal mesh, I think."

"That's . . . good for her, I guess."

"You know what else I heard?"

I suppressed an eye roll, hoping it didn't involve anyone's lady parts since we were eating dinner soon. "No, what?"

"Kim Lockhart was almost an hour late picking her kids up from school the other day and one of the teachers stayed with them until she got there. She smelled so strongly of alcohol that the teacher refused to let the kids go with her. There was a big scene. They had to call her husband to come get her and the kids. You must have met her, she's married to Kyle, the oldest boy."

I remembered meeting Reed's brother and his wife at the barn dance.

"That makes me sad for the kids," I said.

"They have two sweet little guys. I'm sure you know them. Kyle brings them in on occasion for pancakes on Sundays."

"Mama, come see pizza," Noah said. The oven light was on and he was sitting in front of the oven door, watching the pizza cook.

Gene looked down at him with an affectionate smile. Noah didn't have a grandpa, but he had the next best thing in Gene. I sat down next to Noah and we watched as the cheese melted and the crusts browned.

When it was done, we all sat down to dinner. I ate several slices of pizza myself, barely even speaking between bites.

"Nice to see you finally eating," Margie said.

"We were so busy today."

"Busiest diner in all of Missouri, I think," Margie said, with a touch of pride in her voice. I'd grown to realize the difference between Missouri natives and transplants was in the way they pronounced the state name. Margie pronounced it 'Mizzura.' She was definitely a native.

Bedtime for Noah was eight thirty, and once we got the kitchen cleaned up after dinner I settled him into bed. I curled up beside him to help him fall asleep in the double bed we shared in Gene and Margie's guest room. I rubbed circles on his back, feeling my own eyelids drifting closed and, before I knew it, I was fast asleep.

I hadn't had bad dreams for a while but tonight they came back. The nightmare had several variations, and tonight I had the worst one. My father was on top of me, grunting and groaning. Then he disappeared and I looked up from the bed to see my mother looking at me, her mouth set in a thin line of disappointment.

"What have you done, Ivy?" she said. *"Noah deserves better."*

I didn't wake up with a scream, like I sometimes did from these nightmares, but with a huge gasp. I took a deep breath, my heart pounding wildly. When I instinctively reached for Noah, his warmth comforted me. I tucked the covers over his shoulders and smoothed the hair away from his forehead.

My body finally relaxed and I curled back up beside my sleeping son. I didn't think about the past during the day, so why did it come haunt me at night? I thought I'd buried it forever. It took me a while to fall back asleep, but when I did, I slept peacefully until morning. Noah woke me the next morning by holding a forkful of syrup-covered pancake in front of my mouth.

"Eat some pancakes, Mama," he said.

"Hmm?" I opened my eyes and looked at him. "Oh. Morning, buddy."

"Pancakes," he said.

I opened my mouth and let him feed me the bite. He smiled and ran back to Gene and Margie's kitchen.

Noah and I had breakfast with Gene and Margie and then we passed the rest of the weekend with our usual activities—going to the library, doing laundry and cleaning the apartment. Even though the weather was pretty cool, we also visited the park several times so Noah could play on the swings. I loved weekends because I wasn't as exhausted as I often felt on weeknights.

But Monday morning it was back to the grind. I dropped Noah off at daycare, sending him off with several kisses and hugs, and went in for my usual seven to three shift at work.

I worked on autopilot for the first hour, keeping a mental tally of the tips in my pocket. Money was always tight. I bought most of our clothes at garage sales, but the one thing I always splurged on and bought new was shoes, and Noah and I both needed a new pair.

Glancing at my new customer at a small table, I groaned inwardly. Tom Marsh. Or, as the police officer preferred to be called, "Sergeant Marsh." He was a nice enough guy, but he was handsy, and he was getting bolder with time. I preferred to wait on him when he sat at the counter. That way he was on one side and I was on the other side.

"Morning, Sarge," I said, angling myself to face him so he couldn't brush against my ass.

"Ivy." He grinned up at me from his seat and rested a

hand on one of my hips. "Looking gorgeous as always."

"What can I get you to start?" I asked, moving away. "Coffee?"

His unwanted hand on my body made me want to scream inside. I disliked being touched by men, and the fact that he was a cop made it ten times worse.

"Did I hear you're dating one of the Lockhart boys?" He grabbed and squeezed my hip and furrowed his brow, trying to look disappointed. Instead he looked pathetic.

"No, I'm not," I said with disdain in my voice. "Coffee?"

I felt the looks of other customers on us. My tolerance had reached its limit. I turned away and Tom's hand fell away from my hip.

"I'll come back and check on you in a bit," I called over my shoulder.

I went to the pass through in the kitchen to look for my orders and Margie slid in next to me.

"You don't have to let that pervert get touchy-feely, you know. I've told you that. I could tell you were about to deck him."

"I would've enjoyed that," I said, smiling as I remembered Reed's offer to teach me how to box.

"Go take a break outside," Margie said. "I've got your tables."

"I'm fine."

"Go on." She made a shooing motion with her hand. "Get some fresh air."

She knew if I took a break in the kitchen I'd wash dishes or prep for Gene. I found those things relaxing, but Margie always insisted that breaks be work free.

I nodded and headed for the front door. The brisk winter air felt good on my sweaty skin. I was in constant motion at work. It made the time pass quickly and kept me in decent shape. But it also made me feel like a sweaty mess by the end of the work day. My clothes always smelled like greasy diner food, which meant I did, too.

There was a bench around the corner, so I took my apron off and sat down. I wanted to clear away thoughts of Tom and how gross his looks and touches made me feel. With one deep cleansing breath after another, I reminded myself that I wasn't the one who should feel bad.

"Hey, Ivy. How are you?"

I looked up from the bench to see Reed standing several feet away. He wore a dark tailored suit with a bright red tie and a long wool coat. Everything about him was the opposite of a greasy diner waitress.

"I'm good. How about you?"

"Mind if I sit down with you? I'm on my way to the courthouse but I have a little time to spare."

Lovely was the county seat, even though it wasn't the largest town in the county. The old courthouse just off the town square was one of the most beautiful buildings around. Reed could walk there from his nearby office.

"Sure," I said, scooting over.

"Would you like my coat?" he asked. "It's cold out here."

"I'm good. I get hot running around all the time."

Reed nodded and sat down at the other end of the bench. I glanced at the empty space between us. He wasn't like Tom Marsh, who treated women like playthings.

"How was your weekend?" he asked.

"Nice. I made those snowflakes, you know, where you fold up white paper and cut it with scissors and then unfold it?"

He shook his head. "I don't think I ever made those."

"What? I love those things. And when I'd unfold them, Noah would ooh and ahh. So I ended up making like twenty of them and hanging them from our ceiling on strings."

Reed smiled. "Sounds like fun."

"Well, for mommies and toddlers it is," I said, shrugging.

"I would've loved to be there." His warm gaze reminded me of dancing with him at the barn dance. He glanced at his wristwatch and sighed deeply. "I have to get to court, but . . . I wanted to ask you . . . can I take you out this weekend?"

"Out?" I clutched my syrup-stained apron in my hands. "Do you mean like on a date?"

"Yes. I really like you, Ivy."

The hope in his brown eyes crushed me. I'd never been so tempted to accept a date.

"Thank you for asking me," I said. "But I don't date."

He let out a breath and looked at me apologetically. "If I misread the signals, I'm sorry. I didn't mean to make you uncomfortable."

"No, you didn't."

"Didn't . . . on which count?"

I smiled at his cute lawyer speak. "On both counts. You didn't misread the signals or make me uncomfortable."

He turned toward me, his brow furrowed with confusion. "So you like me, but you won't go out with me?"

"I don't date."

"Is it because you don't have a babysitter? Because my mom—"

I shook my head. "It's for other reasons."

A couple seconds of silence passed before he spoke.

"Okay. I respect that." He stood up from the bench. "I have to go, but it's freezing out here. Are you sure you don't want my coat?"

"I'm going back in, but thank you."

He nodded and picked up the briefcase he'd set next to the bench.

"See you at lunch time," I said.

"Sure. Bye, Ivy."

I watched him walk to the courthouse, admiring the lines of his broad shoulders and his tall, athletic frame. I let myself daydream about a date with Reed. To have his full attention for an entire evening would be amazing, no matter what we did. And maybe he'd actually kiss me instead of just saying good night like he had at the barn dance.

Or maybe not, since I'd turned him down.

But I had to stay focused on Noah. Even if I indulged myself in a date, Reed didn't realize who he was asking out. I was so inexperienced I was practically a virgin and I had a deep-seated mistrust of men. I was pretty sure that if I'd accepted, our date wouldn't turn out to be what Reed was expecting.

With a sigh, I stood and went back to work.

Ivy

THE NEXT AFTERNOON, I sat in the pediatrician's office with a drowsy Noah in my arms. His daycare teacher had called me at work to tell me he was running a fever and I'd brought him right over to the doctor.

"Hi Ivy," Dr. Stein said, closing the exam room door

behind him. "What's going on with Noah?"

"He has a fever and a bit of a runny nose. I didn't notice the runny nose this morning but I guess it developed at daycare today."

Dr. Stein scanned his small computer. "Low-grade temp. Let's have a look, Noah."

He checked his ears, nose, throat and chest. Noah, who was half-asleep, didn't protest.

"Just a bit of a cold, I think," Dr. Stein said, returning his stethoscope to its spot around his neck. "Rotate Tylenol and ibuprofen for the fever, give him plenty of liquids and let him rest."

"Okay. Thanks."

"I don't mean to harp, Ivy, but have you checked on your parents' medical records? I've been telling you since Noah was born that given the nature of his paternity, we have to follow him extra close for developmental delays. Knowing his family medical history could be important at some point."

I sighed and looked away. Dr. Stein had delivered Noah, and he was the only one I'd shared the truth with. It was protected medical information and he'd told me I was right to share it since children from parent-child unions had an increased risk of medical problems. He checked Noah thoroughly at every checkup and so far hadn't seen anything abnormal.

"I still haven't contacted my father about it," I admitted.

"I know that is probably something you don't want to face but please do. Noah is perfectly normal from everything I can see. He's even a little ahead on some things. We're past the point of serious concern, but we need to stay tuned in. And family medical history can be critical information for anyone."

"Yes, you're right. I need to get it."

Dr. Stein smiled at me. "You're doing a great job, Ivy. Keep up the good work."

I thanked him and we said goodbye. The thought of reaching out to my father for any reason made me nauseous. But for Noah . . .

Once I got Noah down for a nap at home, I wrote a perfunctory letter to my father. I couldn't bring myself to write the words 'Dear Dad.'

Hi. It's Ivy. My son's pediatrician needs his family medical history. Can you please send yours and anything you know of Mom's? Thanks.

I used the diner's address as my own. Not that he couldn't probably find me if he wanted to, but I couldn't stand the thought of leading him right to my doorstep.

Hopefully he'd send it and that would be that. If he ever came to Lovely, my safe haven, he'd find out his helpless daughter had plenty of fight when it came to protecting her son.

ELEVEN

REED

I PUNCHED AND WOVE to one side, hoping to avoid Mason's blow to my face. But like all the other times he'd hit me since we started boxing almost forty minutes earlier, his reflexes were a little faster than mine.

"Fuck," I muttered when he struck my cheekbone. "Enough."

"Yeah, you had that coming for all your trash talk about kicking my ass," he said, grinning.

"I've always been faster than you." I shook my head as I unlaced a glove with my teeth, confused.

"I still box a couple times a week, though. You're always behind a desk now."

"I lift and work out but, until now, I haven't had anyone to box with."

"I'm happy to help. Besides, you don't have a ball and chain like Kyle and Austin."

"Yeah."

"I'll never understand why they got married so

young. Kim's a fucking nightmare. You think Kyle had some warning she'd end up like this?"

I shook my head. "No way he would've married her if he'd known."

"Monogamy isn't natural," Mason added.

"Kyle loved Kim enough to take a chance, I guess."

"She demanded a bigger wedding ring for their anniversary," Mason said. "Did you hear that? Said it needs to be at least three carats."

I was drinking from a water bottle as he spoke and I choked out a laugh. "A new wedding ring? I didn't even know that was a thing."

"It is for Kim. Sometimes I swear she's trying to push him to divorce her."

"Has to be hard for Kyle, man. They've got kids and he's got a high pressure job."

"Yeah. They're the perfect example of why I might never settle down."

"Me either." I stepped out of the ring and pulled off my sweaty shirt. "Hey, Dad needs us to help him move some bookcases up from the basement at their place. I told him we'd come by when we were done here."

"I think you've had enough ass kicking for today. You ready to go?"

I glared at him. "I'm ready for more anytime."

"Good. You're a good sparring partner for me. Seriously, that was pretty close to a draw."

"It was fun." We headed for the locker room and I turned to my brother. "Hey, you ever teach a woman how to box?"

He snorted a laugh. "No, but it sounds like great foreplay."

An image of a sweaty Ivy, with a gleam of

determination in her blue eyes, made me grin. "Yeah, you might be right."

"Who you wantin' to teach?"

"I don't know," I mumbled dismissively.

"The waitress?"

"Her name's Ivy."

"She's hot."

"Stay away from her," I said, a warning in my tone.

"Easy, little brother. I wouldn't go after any woman you're interested in."

I nodded, took off my sweaty clothes and headed for the shower.

Ivy was on my mind as I lathered soap over my arms and chest. She was on my mind most all the time lately. I kept remembering the way she'd looked sitting next to me on the bench, strands of her dark red hair blowing across her face when a breeze passed.

She'd only said that she didn't date—not that she wasn't interested in me. It didn't feel like a polite brush off. The way she'd turned me down had sounded like she was trying to convince herself as much as me that she didn't date.

I finished my shower and dried off, still thinking about her. She stayed on my mind during the drive to my parents' house and the time spent moving the bookcases.

When I went to the kitchen to get a bottle of water, I leaned against the counter and looked out on the bright sun porch. My gaze went to the spot where Ivy had been sitting when she'd been here a week ago.

"Hi Reed," my mom said as she walked into the kitchen. "You look deep in thought."

I shrugged.

"What's on your mind?" she prodded.

"Ivy."

She nodded and gave me a knowing smile. "I can understand why. She's pretty fantastic, isn't she?"

"Yeah. I asked her out and she shut me down."

"Hmm." Mom furrowed her brow. "Well, if it makes you feel any better, I don't think she dates anyone."

"I know, but . . . I think she's interested in me. And I'm way beyond interested in her. I just don't understand why she won't give me a chance."

"I think she's very protective of her son."

"I'm willing to put in as much time as it takes to earn her trust."

Mom approached and reached up to cup my cheek in her palm. "Sounds like you've got your heart set on her."

"Noah, too. How often does a man get to know a woman's an amazing mother before he's even taken her out on a first date?"

"Well then, I say go for it." She went to the fridge and got out a water for herself.

I sighed with exasperation. "I tried."

"What, asking her out once?" Mom laughed ruefully. "Do you know how many times your father asked me out before I said yes?"

"Sixteen." I'd heard the story many times.

"There are men all over the place looking for sex. Especially in this day and age. If you want something more from Ivy, prove it to her."

I nodded. "I'm not giving up. I just don't know what it'll take to win her over. And . . . crazy as I know it sounds, I think she needs me. Sometimes I see this look in her eyes like . . . she wants something more."

"You'll figure it out. Be patient with her."

I scrubbed a hand down my face, feeling anything

but patient. Seeing Ivy during my weekday lunches at the diner wasn't enough. I wanted her to look up at me like she had that night at the barn dance, questioning whether I was going to kiss her. Only next time, I'd answer her question differently.

Ivy

I DROPPED OFF FOOD for a table of four, tucking my tray under my arm when it was empty. It was lunch hour, and the diner was completely packed. I had lots of customers who should've been on my mind, but only one was commanding my attention.

Tom Marsh hadn't made a single inappropriate comment or tried to rub up against me today. He was probably just in a bad mood. But the way he was watching me from his spot alone at a small table was unnerving.

Every time I glanced over, his eyes were on me. And he didn't have his usual lighthearted smile. He looked intent.

I considered asking Margie to fill his drink and drop off his check. But just a second later I reconsidered. I wouldn't let myself be intimidated.

When I slid his check and a fresh drink onto his table, Tom shifted in his seat and smiled at me.

"You've got a boy, don't you, Ivy?"

His mention of Noah made my skin prickle with nervousness. "Yes."

"And you're all on your own, right? Just you and him."

"I'm not sure what you're getting at." I furrowed my

brow and gave him a *get to the point* look.

"I think you could use a good friend. Someone you could spend some time with and not have the whole town know about it. You know, someone who would help out with money and stuff so you'd have more to spend on your boy."

My stomach rolled with nausea. Was he saying what I thought he was saying?

"I'm a very private person," I said, not knowing how else to respond. "And I really don't have time for friends."

"Everyone needs friends. Don't you think you deserve to be treated special by a man?"

"Uh . . . like I said, I don't have time."

Tom continued in a low tone. "Make time. I'd take real good care of you, Ivy. And no one would need to know."

"This is inappropriate, Tom. So, first of all, the answer is no. And second of all, you're married."

"Get off your high horse." Now his tone was aggravated. "I know you could use some extra money."

His suggestion that I'd sell sex was the last straw. I'd ignored his advances for long enough. He made me feel worse than cheap when he pawed me, stared at my boobs and left me a tip afterwards. He made me feel worthless.

"Go to hell, Tom," I said, narrowing my eyes at him. "Is this the same kind of offer you make to women when you pull them over? Get a ticket or be my friend and I'll get you out of it?"

His expression darkened and he wrapped a hand around my wrist.

"You better watch your mouth," he said ominously.

I laughed humorlessly. "Me?"

"Hey," a deep voice said behind us. I turned to see

Reed approaching quickly, his expression just as pissed off as Tom's. "What the hell is this?"

Reed grabbed Tom's forearm and pushed his hand away from my wrist. He edged himself in front of me so he was between me and Tom. My relief was overshadowed by my embarrassment when other customers turned to see what was going on.

"Nothin,'" Tom said, folding his arms on the table.

"Bullshit." Reed looked at me. "What was he saying to you?"

"I was complaining about my lunch," Tom said. "It's a free country, so I can still do that, can't I?"

"Complain all you want, asshole, but don't fucking touch her."

I'd never seen Reed lose his cool. He was leaning toward Tom, waiting for a response, when Tom jumped up from his seat.

"You want your one o' clock court appearance to be for yourself?" Tom said in a level, challenging tone. "For assaulting a police officer?"

"Bring it. I'd love to tell Judge Tennison I called you an asshole for grabbing a woman who clearly felt threatened by you for no good reason."

"Gentlemen, is there a problem?" Margie asked, approaching and glaring between Reed and Tom.

"I think we're done here," Tom said, tossing a bill on top of his check.

"Did he touch you, Ivy?" Margie asked, turning to me. The entire restaurant was staring at us now.

"Yes." I crossed my arms across my chest. "Today and pretty much every other day he's been in here."

"Douchebag," Reed mumbled.

"Sergeant Marsh, I think you should find another

restaurant to eat at," Margie said.

A hush spread through the diner and Tom widened his eyes incredulously.

"No problem, Margie. You gonna find another police department to call when you have trouble here?"

"I suppose I'll have to take that up with the chief."

Tom shook his head and gave me a dirty look. "You gonna be happy when I get disciplined over this?"

"Get out," Margie said in a raised voice.

Tom started toward the door.

"Shove that badge up your ass," Reed said under his voice. Tom paused for just a second before continuing to the door and walking out.

The tension left the diner with Tom, and customers started buzzing about what they'd just witnessed.

"Did he hurt you?" Reed asked me.

"No."

"What did he say to you?"

I sighed deeply. "He just offered something I'm not interested in."

"What an asshole."

"I'm used to it."

"Other guys put their hands on you here at work?" Reed sounded both angry and surprised.

"I'm a waitress. Men think I'm here to serve them, whether it's breakfast or a little ass grab."

"Well, fuck that. Makes me want to get my laptop and work in here so I can teach them some manners."

This side of Reed was even more charming to me than the polished gentleman I was used to. I touched his shoulder lightly.

"Thanks for standing up for me. I have to get back to work."

"If you have any more problems with him, let me know. Can I give you my number so I know you can reach me if you need to?"

I nodded and he pulled a business card from his pocket, writing on the back of it.

"My cell number." He handed it to me.

"Thanks." I stuck the card in a pocket on my apron.

The excitement in the diner died down and I got back to work. Several customers gave me encouraging smiles to let me know they were on my side. I was more than ready to head home at the end of my shift, but I felt good about standing up for myself with Tom Marsh, and I couldn't help but think about the way Reed and Margie had come to my rescue. I was reminded, again, about how lucky I was to have settled in Lovely.

TWELVE

PROMPTLY AT SEVEN FORTY-FIVE the next morning, Walter slid onto his stool, wearing a scowl. I was there within thirty seconds, knowing how much waiting aggravated him.

"Morning, Walter. What can I get you?"

He eyed me silently. "I've been wondering something. How did a bright young woman like you end up waitressing?"

"So I could get to know charming customers such as yourself."

"I'm serious, Ivy."

"Well, it's seriously none of your business how I came to have this job. Now what'll it be?"

"Don't be so defensive. I see something unfulfilled in you."

I put a hand on my hip and leaned to one side. "Why the sudden interest in me?"

"It's not sudden. I've been coming here every weekday for five months now."

A customer at one of my other tables met my eyes,

sending me a signal for a coffee refill.

"I work here to support my son," I said to Walter. "Now what can I get you?"

"What was your favorite subject in high school?"

"That was forever ago."

"Just humor me, girl. I may be a grouchy old man, but I'm very perceptive. I know you like reading, but when you aren't flipping burgers or changing diapers, what else do you enjoy?"

I laughed humorlessly. Noah and my job were my life. "Uh . . . I don't know."

"Ah." Walter pointed a finger at me. "Now we're getting somewhere. You're red as a ripe tomato. So tell me."

"No. Just order your eggs and toast, please. I have other customers."

He sighed. "Maybe there's nothing there after all."

"Or maybe I don't want to listen to your critical opinions," I snapped.

"So it *is* writing." His smirk was satisfied. "And you're worried the famous author will judge you."

"Well, there certainly aren't any *modest* authors in the room, so I suppose you're right."

"I'm too old to pussy foot around. So what do you write, girl?"

"These days, just orders in this pad right here." I tapped my pen on it for emphasis. "So, what'll it be?"

"Write something and bring it to me. I'll read it and tell you what I think."

I burst out laughing. "No, thanks."

"Opportunity may never knock again." Walter peered at me over the rim of his glasses. "And don't write about the beauty of a flower, or the magic of first love. Write about something that matters. Something that's hard to say. Show me something buried inside you." He scanned the menu, his moment of humanity passing. "Two eggs, over medium. Wheat toast with real butter. Small dish of plain oatmeal."

I took the menu he held out and hustled to grab a fresh pot of coffee. Walter had to be experiencing a moment of temporary insanity. He couldn't possibly see something unfulfilled in the waitress who delivered his coffee and eggs every morning, and collected his fifteen percent tip.

I'd loved writing in high school, but I wouldn't be sharing that information with a rich, famous author who was so critical he could bring down your mood with just a glance. Walter would have to settle for judging my waitressing skills rather than my writing ability.

For the rest of my shift I tried to keep my mind on taking orders, delivering food and maximizing my tips with fast service. But my thoughts kept wandering back to Walter's offer, and his comment about seeing something unfulfilled in me.

Why had I given up writing? My high school ACT test scores had been very good, but not exceptional. I knew in my heart that it was the essay I'd written about my mother's death that had won me the Stanford scholarship. I could hide my truths from others, and even from myself, by pushing aside painful memories. But there was something about writing that forced me to pour out my raw feelings.

Maybe that was why it was hard to think about picking up a pen again. I still wasn't ready to confront the darkness that had changed the course of my life.

When my shift ended, I was drawn to stop by the library and email April. Lillian wasn't at the desk so I sat down, opened my email and started typing.

> *Dear April,*
>
> *I wish you weren't so far away. It would be good to talk to you about something in person, but e-mail will have to do.*
>
> *There's an author here in Lovely who is one of my customers at the diner. He's kind of an old grouch, but I can't help liking him. He said he sees something unfulfilled in me and somehow got me to admit I used to like writing. Then he said I should write something and he'll judge it for me.*
>
> *The thought of writing again is so scary to me. Not because I have nothing to say, but because I do. Does that make sense at all?*
>
> *Also, a guy asked me out. Not just any guy, either. He's tall, dark and way beyond handsome. He's the one who caught me that day when I slipped and fell. His name is Reed, and he's everything I'm not. He's an attorney who grew up in Lovely and he has a perfect, huge, close-knit family. He's straightforward and sweet. Also, he smells amazing. That's an insignificant detail, but I thought you should know.*
>
> *Sounds great, right? So of course I said no. I don't know how to go on a date with a man like him. And what if he found out about my past?*
>
> *I just looked at the time and I have to go. Hopefully all this will pass and I can get back to my quiet, peaceful life. But, having said that, I would sure love to get your take on things.*
>
> *Miss you,*
> *xo Ivy*

THE NEXT DAY I was leaving work an hour early to volunteer at craft time in Noah's daycare class when Margie stopped me.

"Something came in the mail for you," she said, handing me an envelope, her eyes narrowed in confusion. "Michigan postmark."

My heart thumped hard in my chest as I took the letter and put it in my purse. "Thanks, Margie. I've gotta go, but I'll see you in the morning." I dashed out of the diner before Margie had a chance to ask the questions I knew were forming in her mind.

I rushed to my car and tore into the envelope, praying he'd sent the information I'd asked for. There was a hand-written letter and attached to it were two fully completed medical forms.

Closing my eyes, I sighed with relief. Part of me wanted to shred the letter without even reading it, but curiosity got the better of me.

Dear Ivy,

After more than three years, you send nothing but a request for medical information? I think you owe me more than that. I've never even met my grandson.

I wish you wouldn't have left without talking to me, but I'm not mad anymore. All I want is to put the past behind us and find a way to get to know each other again.

You know how to reach me. Better yet, come home for a visit. It would be great to see you.

Love,
Dad

I slammed my hand on the steering wheel of my car, angry tears welling over. My disgust and anger toward him had reached a new level.

I owed him? He wasn't mad anymore? Come home for a visit?

Gripping the steering wheel with all my strength, I rested my head on it and tried to force away the rage that was consuming me. I had to pull myself together. I was expected at Noah's school in fifteen minutes and I couldn't show up there upset and crying.

With a deep breath, I put the papers back in the envelope and buried it in my purse. Later I'd find a cathartic way to destroy his letter. Maybe I'd cut it into pieces and burn them individually.

He wasn't even sorry. I knew deep down that if he was, he'd have found a way to contact me and say it. But even when opportunity was staring him in the face, he'd tried to make it out like we were estranged over some insignificant teenage hissy fit.

Damn him. Not just for what he did, but for how he could still make me feel. I started the car, forcing away thoughts of him. That was my only way forward—bury the past and take on the future, one step at a time.

REED

I WALKED INTO MY office and flipped on the lights. I'd been composing an email to another attorney in my head and I wanted to get it typed and sent immediately. But the email was forgotten when I saw the stack of dark brown boxes in the corner of my office.

"What in the . . . ?" I stuck my head through the open doorway and called down the hallway. "Lena, what's all this?"

"Bart Daniels had them dropped off. They're the files for some cases he said you'd be helping with as assistant public defender."

I stared at the five foot tall stack of boxes. When I'd agreed to be assigned assistant public defender, I'd figured it would be a few overflow cases, and anything Bart was unable to take on due to a conflict of interest.

Maybe the boxes weren't full. Well, other than the two on bottom, which had files bulging out the sides. I walked over to the boxes and pulled the lid from the one on top.

Shit. The box was stuffed full.

With a deep sigh, I took my jacket off and rolled up my shirt sleeves. I'd fire off that email and then I'd sort through the files and see how many cases I had to get up to speed on. There would be a hell of a lot of cases, I already knew that. Good thing I was still young and eager.

Ivy

MY CELL PHONE BUZZED from the pocket of my apron. I pulled it out and glanced at the screen. A voicemail from April. She must have read my e-mail and decided to call instead of emailing. I'd have to call her back this evening when I was off work.

I stuck the phone back in my pocket and returned to work. A few minutes later I saw a tall man walk into the diner, just catching his frame out of the corner of my eye.

I couldn't help looking up—it was Reed. He gave me a grin that made me smile so wide I bit my lip in an effort to contain it.

Forcing myself to focus on my customers, I finished taking their order. Reed was sitting in my section, so I walked over to his table.

"Hi there," I said. "What can I get you to drink?"

"Hey," he said softly. "Can I just tell you that I spent the whole morning going through files? Hundreds of 'em. My office looks like a paper factory exploded in it."

"That doesn't sound good," I said, laughing.

"It's not. But you know why I was in a good mood the whole time I sorted through that mess of paperwork?"

The gleam in his eye made me warm inside. "I can't imagine."

"Because I knew I was gonna come here for lunch and see you. And, even better, ask you a certain question again." He put his arm around the vacant chair next to his and sprawled out comfortably.

"You're asking me out again?"

"I like you too much not to. And if you turn me down, I'll just ask again."

"Reed . . ."

"What do I need to do to convince you to give me a chance?"

"I don't—"

"You want me to serenade you in front of this entire diner full of people?" He stood up and grinned at me. "Because I will."

I bit my lip to avoid laughing at the image. "No, that won't be—"

He got down on one knee in front of me and I gave him a puzzled look.

"Why do you build me up?" he belted out. "Buttercup—"

"No! Reed, get up." My face warmed with nervous embarrassment.

Customers were giving us looks of amusement.

"She won't go out with me," Reed explained to the couple at a nearby table.

"Reed Lockhart, you're out of your mind," I murmured.

"Tell me what I have to do. There has to be a way I can convince you. One date, Ivy, that's all I ask."

I scanned the diner, trying to think of an answer. My gaze landed on my most crotchety customer, who was here for a rare lunch.

"You have to convince Walter," I said.

"What?"

I smiled as the idea took root in my head. "Convince Walter to tell me to go out with you, and I will."

Reed rolled his eyes and blew out a breath. "I don't think I could convince him to piss on me if I was on fire."

"You're a lawyer. Isn't convincing your thing?"

His lips turned up in a smile. "It's *one* of my things, Miss Gleason. So if I can persuade Walter, you'll let me take you out?"

"Yes. I might even consider wearing something nicer than these old jeans. That is, *if* you can convince him."

"You make those jeans look good." He considered for a second. "Okay. I accept this challenge."

I nodded and tried to look nonchalant, though my heart was pounding. "I have to get back to work."

"Keep Friday night open." He gave me one more smile before turning toward Walter.

I wanted to eavesdrop, but I had tables on the other

side of the diner. As I walked over there, I found myself actually hoping Walter was in a good mood today.

THIRTEEN

REED

WALTER GRIEVES GLARED AT me over the top of his glasses.

"Mr. Grieves," I said, extending a hand. "Reed Lockhart."

"What do you want, Mr. Lockhart?" He ignored my hand and I dropped it.

"Well, I want to take Ivy Gleason out on a date."

"And that has what to do with me? Talk quickly, my soup's getting cold."

I gave him my best disarming smile. "She must think a lot of you, sir, because she turned me down the first time I asked, but the second time she told me that if I can convince you to tell her she should go out with me, then she will."

His eyes sparkled with amusement, but his scowl remained in place. "Is that right? Well, unfortunately for you, I think a lot of her as well. And you look like a man who's thinking with the wrong head for me to even consider endorsing the idea of a date with her."

"How do you figure that?" I gave him a skeptical look. "I'm respectable and I'm wearing a suit."

Walter turned to me, the lines of his scowl deepening. "It's not your clothes. It's the way you stare at her like you're starving and she's dinner."

Defensiveness kicked in. "I don't stare at her like that. I really like Ivy. I'm not after what you think I am."

He grunted dismissively. "No. She's a nice girl and I don't want her getting hurt."

"I won't hurt her."

"My soup is probably icy cold now, because you won't accept the answer I'm giving." He narrowed his eyes at me. "Let's see . . . expensive suit, sense of entitlement and a recalcitrant attitude. You must be an attorney."

I scoffed and blew out a breath, unsure how to respond.

"That's right, young man. And don't try to evade the question. Are you an attorney?"

"Yes, sir," I said, meeting his eyes as my chances of a date with Ivy this weekend sailed out the window.

"Then not only no, but hell no. Now, please leave me to my lunch."

Walter turned around and I headed back for my table, stealing a glance at Ivy who was delivering food to a table. Damn. It would take a miracle to change his mind. But I wasn't giving up. I needed to think about things before approaching him again.

Ivy

I STILL FELT A warm glow from seeing Reed at lunch. Margie had delivered his food before I had a chance to grab it, so I hadn't gotten a chance to talk to him again. But from what I'd seen of the conversation between him and Walter, it hadn't gone well.

Just knowing he was interested in me was enough. It made me feel pretty in a way I'd never felt before and not like a piece of ass. Reed was handsome and smart and sweet, and when he looked at me, I felt . . . worthy.

The end of my shift was just a few minutes away and I was cleaning behind the front counter when Larry Waters, the Lovely Police Chief, approached and waved me over.

"You want a carryout order, Chief?" I asked, pulling out my order pad.

"No." He glanced from side to side before continuing. "I'm here to say I'm real sorry about what happened with Sergeant Marsh. I talked to several witnesses and he's been suspended pending a review of his employment by the Police Commission."

"He might get fired?" I shook my head. "If he doesn't come in here anymore, that's enough for me. I don't expect him to get in trouble at work."

"Is it true that he's touched you inappropriately?"

I looked off to the side and sighed. "Inappropriate means different things to different people."

"In any way that was unwanted by you. That would be inappropriate."

"Yeah, but it's not like he's the only one. It kind of goes with the territory of being a waitress."

"It sure as hell doesn't have to. If this happens with any customer—anyone at all—you tell him no, and if it happens again, you call me."

I nodded silently.

"Police officers have to conform to a higher standard, Ivy," he continued. "We're in a position of trust. Would it be okay for me to interview you down at the station about how Sergeant Marsh has touched you and any unwelcome comments he's made?"

"I don't know. I try to keep a very low profile, and the last thing I need is a police officer mad at me."

"You let me worry about that. This behavior is often a pattern. You might be protecting another woman from unwanted advances or something even worse."

Tears welled in my eyes as the past pushed its way into my consciousness. Should I have turned my father in for what he did to me? Keeping it a secret had seemed like the only way I could survive it. In a lot of ways, it still did. I'd reinvented myself in Lovely. Here, I was a single mom who worked and kept to herself. That was who I wanted to be. I couldn't become a woman whose child was her half-brother. And more importantly, Noah didn't deserve the stigma the truth would bring. He was completely innocent. I'd protect him from anything.

Though I couldn't tell anyone what my father had done, I could be honest about Tom. And it was hard to refuse the chief, who was looking at me earnestly.

"Okay," I said, taking a deep breath and wiping the tears from my cheeks. "I'll come in and talk to you."

We agreed on a day and time and the chief handed me a slip of paper with the appointment written on it. I went back to work, but my emotions were still running high.

It wasn't Tom Marsh I was upset about, but my father. He'd put me in an impossible position. Turn him in and tell the world my son was the product of an incestuous sexual assault, or keep it secret and let him get away with it.

My hands shook as I washed dishes at the end of my shift. I'd asked to get off the floor because I couldn't bear talking to customers right now.

Picking up Noah and spending time with him should have relaxed me. But looking into his big innocent eyes made me more resentful toward my father than ever. My son wouldn't have a daddy to play ball with him. He'd miss out on so much. Then there was the added worry of health problems because he was technically inbred. My beautiful son being labeled with something so ugly was brutally unfair. Noah deserved everything good.

I didn't call April back, because I was so upset I was liable to blurt out the whole truth to her. She suspected I'd been sexually assaulted and had encouraged me to get counseling shortly after I arrived in Lovely. I'd spoken to someone for a couple months, never telling the complete truth. It had helped some, but the demons were never far away.

I hugged Noah close until he fell asleep, but I was too emotional to sleep myself. I crept out of bed and sat down on the couch with an empty notebook and pen.

Dear Brad,

I'll never call you Dad again. As a father you are dead to me. I figured I was dead to you, too, until I received your letter.

You want to meet your grandson? You have no grandson. You have no daughter. You have no one and nothing, and you're too arrogant to realize it's your own fault.

What you did to me was unimaginable. You took away my belief in the goodness of people. You took away my ability to trust. Your own sexual gratification meant more to you than the daughter who was still grieving her mother's death.

Drunk or not, what you did was wrong. And the horror I couldn't imagine back then is all too familiar now. I relive what you did in nightmares that leave me shaking and crying.

My letter was not an attempt to get back in touch with you. I only wanted the medical information the doctor needs about my son.

Why can't you bring yourself to say it? You raped me. My son will never have a father because the sick, twisted truth is that if he had one, it would be you.

You disgust me. I hate you. I wish there was a way for me to hurt you as much as you hurt me. I believe there's a special place in hell for you. It's reserved for men worse than those who rape their daughters. This place is for men who do it and aren't even sorry.

Rot there.

Ivy

My notebook was filled with crossed out words and rewrites, so I penned a final draft and re-read it. I tore it out, folded it and put it in an envelope.

My hand shook as I took it to work the next morning. I was so afraid of what he would say.

But it wasn't my father I was worried about—he'd never see this letter. It was Walter. I left the envelope next to his breakfast spot.

He wanted me to write about something that mattered and I had. Whether he liked it or not, I felt stronger for having written it. I'd finally put into words the feelings that had been buried in me for so long.

REED

FOR THE THIRD DAY in a row, I was waiting in the seat next to Walter's when he arrived for breakfast at seven forty-five.

"Morning, Mr. Grieves," I said.

He grunted with disapproval. "If you think you can annoy me into changing my mind, think again."

Ivy approached and poured coffee into his mug.

"Good morning, Walter." She pulled out her order pad. "I see you've got company again."

"Yes, much to my dismay. It's bad when a man can't even have his breakfast in peace." The words were grumpy, but there was a twinkle in his eyes.

Ivy tried to hide a smile. "Well, what can I get you?"

He rattled off his usual order and Ivy caught my eye before she walked away.

"She's the most beautiful woman I've ever seen," I said to Walter. "It's not the beauty you see in magazines or on TV. It's something very rare. I can tell when I say something that makes her happy because her eyes just shine."

Walter ignored me, scanning the pages of the newspaper, but I continued.

"You know, as crazy as this sounds, I think I'm in love with her."

He pretended to ignore me, but I saw his eyes widen. Walter was listening, alright.

"I know right when it happened, too," I said. "I remember feeling like my chest just wasn't big enough for my heart in that moment. I saw her at Jimmy's Italian Place with her son. The looks on their faces . . . it was pure, unconditional love. I could feel her devotion to him. She has a good heart, and that's where her beauty comes from."

"Well, you're a real poet," he muttered.

I shrugged. "It's the truth. I'll be sitting here at seven forty-five for as many days as it takes to convince you. She's worth it."

He mumbled something, but I missed it. I was too busy watching Ivy making coffee. It was a simple task, but her long, graceful fingers made it captivating. Her hair was pulled back in a ponytail, and I imagined myself releasing it to let it fall around her shoulders, and then burying my face in it.

I'd been adamant about not falling for a woman in Lovely when I moved back. But I'd had no say in the matter. Ivy had grabbed my attention at Gene's Diner, mesmerized me at a barn dance and stolen my heart at Jimmy's Italian Place.

It was love, Lovely style. Now I just needed her to feel the same way about me.

Ivy

BY THE END OF my shift, my back ached. The new waitress had decided to quit by not showing up this morning, and we'd all had to pull extra weight. And my extra weight had been literal. I'd rotated supplies in the walkin cooler so the new deliveries were placed in the back allowing us to use stuff in the order it had come in. The job was usually done by Gene or Shawn, but Gene hadn't been able to get out from behind the grill all day, and Shawn had been bussing tables nonstop, so I'd stayed an hour after my shift to get it done.

When I finally walked outside the winter air felt good. I took in a deep breath and blew it out, a visible cloud appearing in front of my mouth.

"Ivy," a male voice said.

I jumped with surprise as I turned.

"Walter." I laughed lightly. "You scared me."

"I just wanted a chance to talk to you when you're not working," he said. "Can we take a short walk?"

I looked him over as I nodded. He wore a dark newsboy hat and a matching wool trench coat, his hands stuffed in the pockets. I found him a little intimidating. Right now, he seemed a lot more like a famous author than my grouchy customer.

"I read your letter," he said, looking straight ahead as we walked down one side of the downtown square. "May I ask if it was fact or fiction?"

I zipped up my sweatshirt to ward off the cold. "Fact."

A few moments of silence passed before Walter spoke.

"I'd first like to say how sorry I am for what happened to you."

I stared at the cars moving in the distance, unable to look at Walter.

"I didn't write it because I wanted your sympathy."

Walter chuckled beside me. "I realize that. Do you ever think about the fact that every person has his own story? Like that fellow over there." He nodded toward a man on the other side of the square who was walking briskly, his head bowed. "He could be fighting some inner battle we'll never know about."

"That's true."

"My wife left me after our daughter died," he said. "I didn't know how to cope. I started drinking. When she needed me most, I wasn't there. It's something I'll always have to carry with me."

"I don't know what to say, Walter. I'm so sorry about your daughter."

He shook his head as we turned a corner. "No one forgets their darkest moments, Ivy. Just like you can't forget it, neither can he. He'll carry the shame until he takes his last breath. Nothing you could ever do or say could hurt like the truth he has to live with. Now, that's not meant to minimize what you feel, because you're very entitled to those feelings. I just want you to know that pain can seem inescapable, but it isn't. Guilt, however, is inescapable."

"He should feel guilty."

"Damn right. And you should feel like a survivor."

"I do."

"After I read what you wrote, I went into my office and wrote for ten hours straight." He laughed softly. "I haven't done that in years. Do you know why I did it?"

I shook my head silently.

"Because you moved me, Ivy. With the raw honesty

of your words. I felt the pain in that letter."

I swallowed hard, pleased by the compliment. "I couldn't think of anything else to write about."

"Ah. Because those are strong feelings. How in the hell *could* you write about a tree or your favorite vacation when you've got that inside you?"

I smiled. Walter stopped at a bench in the park and gestured for me to sit down beside him.

"Putting things into words is cathartic, no?" he said.

"Very much. I should send him the letter, but . . . I'm not there yet."

"Keep writing, Ivy. You have a leg up on other writers. You've experienced the depths of loss and hurt and love. Through not just your mother's loss and what your father did, but the joy you experience through your son. Use those things. Draw on them and show others they aren't alone. Tell stories that matter. Fiction is about characters who don't exist, but their pain and sorrow and joy are very real."

"I wanted to major in English in college but I wasn't able to go."

Walter furrowed his brow and looked at me over the thick rims of his glasses. "My books had made me seven figures before I went back and finished my degree. The only thing that can keep you from writing is you. Don't let that happen."

His words warmed me. "Okay. I won't let that happen. Thank you, Walter."

"And now we need to talk about the Lockhart boy," he said, his grumpy tone returning.

"Reed?"

"I think that's the one who's been pestering me to convince you to go on a date with him."

I laughed. "Sorry. I had to tell him something, and I figured you'd chase him off."

Walter eyed me over the rims of his glasses again. "Because going out with an attractive, intelligent man who is obviously ass over teakettle for you would be so awful?"

I sighed deeply. "Well, now you know why, Walter. I closed myself off a long time ago."

"You may have, but you're fighting your way back."

I gave him a skeptical glance.

"Ivy, as long as you keep your feelings deep inside, your father wins. You're letting it come to the surface because you want more than that now. Let the anger and betrayal boil over and you'll feel stronger. You'll *be* stronger. All this time, you've survived, and I admire you for that. But maybe it's time to do more than survive."

"You're telling me to go out with Reed?"

"I think you'd be crazy not to. I really believe he's going to ask me every day for as long as it takes. He's persistent, loyal and protective. And from what I know of them, the Lockharts are good people."

"I think so, too."

"So open up and try it."

I wrapped my arms around myself, feeling excited by the prospect.

"Walter, I feel like I'm the one who owes you a tip this time."

"I won't disagree."

"Just don't expect more than fifteen percent."

FOURTEEN

I RAN MY FINGERS over the small silver butterfly pendant on the necklace my mom gave me for my sixteenth birthday. I hadn't looked at it since before she died. It had been tucked away in its box which, in turn, was wrapped up in a scarf, in a drawer of my dresser.

It was time to wear it again.

When I'd dropped Noah off at Margie and Gene's earlier, she'd given me a gift box from a downtown boutique.

"I wanted you to have something new to wear tonight," she said as she handed it to me after work. The hopeful, happy look in her eyes had made my throat tight.

Inside the box was an emerald green, cashmere V-neck sweater. It was more beautiful than anything I'd ever owed. I cried and then Margie did, too. Even Gene's eyes looked misty.

When I got home and put the sweater on over a white cotton camisole with my favorite old jeans, I felt beautiful. Not just because of the sweater, but because Margie gave it to me out of love. Whether or not any of us said it out loud, she and Gene were family to me and Noah. They'd never had children of their own, and I knew we'd found our way to each other for a reason.

Since I had a token from Margie to wear on my date with Reed, it seemed right to wear the necklace, too.

I called April, but she didn't answer so I left a message telling her I was going on a date. I knew she'd be happy and that she'd call tomorrow expecting details.

A knock sounded at the door and my stomach flipped over nervously. I took a deep breath, squared my shoulders and made the short trip from the bedroom to the door. When I opened it, Reed stood there smiling at me.

"Hey," he said.

"Hi." I tucked my hair behind my ear nervously. "I'm ready. I just need to get my coat and purse."

I closed the door and turned to grab my stuff from the couch. A soft knock on the door made me open it up immediately.

"What's wrong?" I asked, looking at Reed through the crack of light filtering in.

"Uh . . ." He gave me a lopsided grin. "Can I come in? I wanted to, um—"

I opened the door all the way, seeing the long white box in his arms for the first time.

"Oh. What's that?"

He pulled off the lid, revealing a dozen long-stemmed red roses.

"Oh my God." I met his eyes with surprise. "Reed, you didn't have to do that. No one's ever given me flowers. Unless a junior prom corsage counts." I laughed nervously.

"Can I bring them inside?"

I stepped aside. "You can, but . . . my place isn't much.

You probably guessed that based on the proximity to the railroad tracks. And the missing siding on the outside of the building."

"Ivy." Reed stepped inside and looked around. "Don't be nervous, okay? Your place is great."

He looked around the living room, which consisted of a threadbare green couch with a blanket covering the cushions, a coffee table and pictures of me and Noah on the walls. I'd also framed several pictures he'd drawn or painted.

I reached for the box in his arms. "I guess I should put these in water, right? I don't have a vase, but maybe I've got something else that will work."

The kitchen was just a few feet away, and I stepped into it and looked through my cabinets, my heart pounding in my chest. I hadn't been alone with a man since . . .

I couldn't think about that. Not now. I'd think about the sweater and the necklace and Reed, who had just brought me a dozen red roses.

My kitchen was filled with practical essentials. I didn't own a single item that red roses would look pretty in. But I had to make something work.

There was an empty milk jug on the counter, waiting to be taken out to the trash. I grabbed it and rinsed it out in the sink. After I cut the top of it off to make room for the stems, it looked . . . hideous, but it was all I had.

I trimmed the ends of the roses, filled the empty jug with water and arranged the flowers in it. When I put it in the center of my small, scratched up kitchen table, I heard Reed laughing softly.

"Clever," he said.

"Thank you for the roses. They're beautiful."

"You're welcome. You look gorgeous, by the way."

My cheeks warmed as he looked at me. "I was hoping jeans would be okay."

"Perfect." He reached his hand out to me. "Are you all set?"

I took his hand and we walked out together after I grabbed my coat and purse, bundling it up under one arm so I could keep my hand in his.

For nearly four years now my gut had told me not to let men touch me. I wasn't sure if it was my heart or my gut telling me now that Reed was different, and that I didn't need to worry. Much as I wanted to be a strong, independent woman who didn't need anyone but Noah, this felt good. When Reed opened the passenger door to his dark pickup truck, he kept hold of my hand while I stepped inside.

"Where are we going?" I asked.

His expression turned sheepish and he smiled. "Have you ever been to Stumpy's?"

"No, but I think I've driven past it. Stumpy's Supper Club?"

"Yeah. It looks like a dive, but the food's the best."

"Is Stumpy the owner?"

"Yeah. I don't even know his real name. He started going by Stumpy after he lost his hand to a wood chipper."

"That's terrible."

"I'm failing at romantic date talk here, aren't I?" he said, grinning. "Stumpy's the happiest guy you'll ever meet. I think you'll like his place."

Reed closed my door and I watched him walk around the front of the truck to the driver's side. He wore jeans and a navy blue sweater with a white dress shirt beneath. It was the best of both his sides. I liked rugged Reed from the barn dance, in jeans, a flannel shirt and boots, the best. But I also appreciated the way he looked in the suits that fit the lines of his large frame just right.

He got in the truck and had just started it when I blurted, "I haven't been on a date in more than four years."

His lips parted for just a moment, like he was about to speak. Instead, I continued. "I just . . . wanted you to know. My last date was in high school, and it was probably a trip to the Shack O' Shakes for some ice cream. I've never been on an adult date. I'm kinda nervous."

"The Shack O' Shakes?" Reed arched his brows and smiled. "That sounds like a hometown favorite."

"Kind of a tie with the Double Dipper," I admitted.

"And what town was this in? Where'd you grow up?"

I looked away from him. "It's a town in Michigan. A place of bad memories that I'd like to forget."

"Consider it forgotten." He put his hand on the back of my seat as he looked over his shoulder to back out.

We made small talk about Noah and his parents as he drove. I kept my hands in my lap, where I hoped Reed couldn't see me squeezing them together so hard my knuckles turned white.

The gravel parking lot of Stumpy's was so full when we arrived that Reed had to park in the grass. When we walked in to the dimly-lit restaurant, the savory smell of grilling steak made me remember how hungry I was.

A greeter led us to a wooden booth in a corner and Reed hung our coats on an ornate hook that adorned a rustic wood post next to our table. A waitress approached and we both ordered water.

"So," Reed said when we were alone again. "You grew up in Michigan, and you like to dance. Tell me something else about you."

I considered. "Hmm . . . well, I once won a spelling bee by spelling the word ambidextrous."

"How old were you?"

"I was in fifth grade."

"So you're smart. I already knew that, though."

I gave him a skeptical glance. "How would you know that?"

"You finally said yes to a date with me." He grinned and I laughed at his sheepish expression. "Seriously, tell me about yourself."

I shrugged. "I grew up in Michigan, as you know. My mom was a stay at home mom and my dad was a sheriff's deputy. I'm an only child. I was planning to go to Stanford and major in English, but then I had Noah, so . . . there was change of plans."

"Are you still in touch with his father?"

I shook my head. "It's just me and Noah."

"What about your parents? Do they ever visit?"

"My mom died when I was eighteen. And I don't have anything to do with my dad anymore."

"I'm sorry about that, Ivy."

I shrugged. "I have Noah. He's enough."

The waitress returned with our water, a basket of bread and a big salad. I sipped from my glass and buttered a piece of bread, feeling self-conscious as I felt Reed's intense gaze on me.

"You're looking at me," I said. "It makes me feel like maybe I have food in my teeth or something."

"No," he said, smiling. "There's just nothing else here I'd rather look at."

My cheeks warmed and I cleared my throat. "So, will you tell me more about you? I know you're an attorney from a family with a crazy good gene pool and that you were once engaged. What else?"

"A good gene pool, huh?" Reed arched his brows with amusement.

"Well, look at you. All five of you. I assume your other brother's attractive even though I've never met him."

Reed shook his head. "He's a troll."

"I doubt that."

"More about me . . ." he said, seeming to think about it. "You know I love basketball and boxing. I've got a black lab. I like to cook." He shrugged as if to say, 'That's about it.'

"Why'd you move back home?"

"The short answer is to help out with my dad's practice. He's getting older and wants to slow down soon."

I'd never been drunk. But sitting across from Reed with no distractions, his brown eyes focused on me, made me feel intoxicated. I wasn't sure how long I just looked at him before speaking again.

"So, what's the long answer?"

"You want the long answer?" he asked, grinning.

"Something tells me it's the more interesting one."

"Okay." He rubbed the dark stubble on his chin. "I did a paper in law school about the disproportionate number of minorities and poor people who are arrested in the US. It sparked my interest, so I started volunteering at a place that provides legal aid in St. Louis. Lovely is the county seat in one of the most poverty-stricken counties in the state. I came home because I want to start a non-profit here to provide legal aid."

"Wow." I sat back in my seat, studying him. "That's amazing."

"I haven't been able to start anything yet because I'm so busy at my dad's office and with my public defender cases. I'll have to apply for grants and have some of them come through to get it off the ground."

A couple hours passed as we ate steak and baked potatoes and then talked until Stumpy's started clearing out. Reed was careful to avoid questions about my parents. We talked about favorite books and movies, the places we dreamed of traveling and the music we both loved. It might have seemed like innocuous conversation, but it told me a lot about him. His love of Monty Python was proof of his good sense of humor. His dream vacation of pub-hopping in Ireland told me he wasn't pretentious.

I didn't want the date to end but eventually we did have to leave. We slowly walked out to his truck, and when we got to the passenger door, we both stood there, neither of us making a move to open it. I let my back rest against the door, looking up at the shadows cast on his face in the darkness of the parking lot.

He put his hands on my hips, his touch igniting me. The warmth radiating from him wasn't just physical. His dark, coffee-colored eyes were full of longing and emotion.

When he leaned down, a thrill of anticipation coursed through me. He was going to kiss me. I wanted it more than my next breath, but at the same time, the charge of electricity in the air was overwhelming.

This wouldn't be *just* a kiss. It would change everything. I'd no longer be a woman who could turn down a date with him. Instead, I'd be completely smitten with this tall, dark handsome man. He'd have me on a string. And the intensity I saw in his gaze told me I'd have him on one as well.

I'd never felt wanted like this. It was exhilarating and terrifying. What would Reed say when he found out I was practically a virgin? And worse, what would be say if he found out my father was also Noah's father?

I couldn't stomach the thought of Reed being disgusted with me. Though I'd done nothing wrong, the truth of what happened was still shocking and disturbing.

My protective instinct kicked in.

"I'm not . . . what you want, Reed," I said, shaking my head.

"Why would you say that?"

"I have my reasons, but it's private. Just trust me. A woman like . . . whatever her name is . . . your ex—she's better for you than I am."

"Are you in love with someone?"

"No. Not even close. Unless Noah counts."

"I'm not interested in Meredith. It's you I want."

"You say that, but—"

"I said it because I mean it."

I balled my hands into fists, frustrated but not sure what to do about it.

"You don't even know what you're saying," I said. "When there's a physical attraction for one person and something more for the other, that's a recipe for disaster."

He furrowed his brow, looking like he was trying not to smile. "Which person am I in this scenario? Are you saying you only want me for my body?"

"No. The other way around."

Reed tightened his hold on my waist, closing the distance between us. My soft body molded against his powerful one in all the right places—my nipples tightening against his chest and his erection hard against my stomach.

"So you're not interested in my body?" he asked with a mock frown.

His light tone caught me off guard and I laughed and laid a palm on his chest. "I didn't say that."

"I hope you know I'd never ask out a single mom unless I had no choice."

I arched my brows, amused. "No choice?"

"No choice. You cast a spell over me, Ivy. I was interested after we danced that night, but then I saw you with Noah at Jimmy's, and . . . you had me. I felt like I could see into your heart, and what I saw was . . . everything I could ever want. So much goodness and beauty."

His words wrapped around my heart, drawing me in even further than a kiss may have.

"But . . . does it bother you that I have a son?"

"Not at all. But he's part of this, too. I'm not gonna lie and say I've never wanted a woman for just sex. But I'd never do that to a woman with a child. I wouldn't have asked you out if I didn't have strong feelings for you."

"I feel like . . . if you kiss me, things will never be the same."

He leaned his forehead down against mine. "They won't. But that's a good thing, Ivy."

"So do it, then." I wrapped my hands around his biceps, the hard lines of muscle beneath his shirt making my core tingle with a warm, pleasant ache. "Kiss me."

"I will." He squeezed my waist, pulling me tightly against him. "But not yet."

I leaned back and glared at him. "Reed. You're a tease."

He laughed deeply, looking up at the sky for a second. "Now there's something I've never been called."

"It's true."

"I'm enjoying this," he said, taking my hand. "Seeing you so eager for a kiss. And there's only one first one. So be patient and I'll make it worth your wait."

He reached next to me and opened the door of the truck. I stepped in, surprised that I was once again disappointed he hadn't kissed me.

I studied his profile as he drove back to my apartment. His defined jaw line and large shoulder were easy to stare at.

"Thank you for tonight," I said. "I loved it."

He glanced over at me and grinned. "Me too. When can I take you out again?"

"Depends on how that kiss goes."

His deep laugh made my stomach flip nervously. It was my first date in more than four years, and I was so glad I'd finally taken a chance. I'd convinced myself that I didn't want to feel desired by a man ever again. But with Reed, it was a feeling I couldn't get enough of.

Butterflies were clamoring in my stomach when Reed parked in front of my apartment and walked me to the door.

I unlocked it and looked up at him. "Do you want to come in for a bit?"

"Yeah, I do. That's why I'm not going to."

He smoothed a strand of hair back from my face and leaned down, his fingers grazing across my jaw line. When his lips met mine, my heart pounded so hard I wondered if he could feel it through my chest. His lips were soft and slow and gentle, seeming to savor mine. Then he slid his hand around to the back of my neck, his tongue brushing across mine in a way that made me moan against him.

I held onto his jacket, feeling dizzy. When he pulled his mouth away from mine, I instinctively leaned up and kissed him. He groaned softly and wrapped his arms around my waist, pulling me against him.

I felt his desire in the kiss and in his evident arousal, which was again pressed against my belly. This time when Reed moved his lips away, he trailed them down my jaw line to my neck. I gasped from the warmth of his mouth and the brush of his stubble on the sensitive skin of my neck.

"I should go," he whispered in my ear.

I nodded, unable to think straight. This was good . . . more than good, actually. It was better than I'd ever thought a kiss could feel. Every inch of my body was on fire for Reed.

"Next weekend," I said, reaching up to touch his scruffy cheek.

"Hmm?"

"Another date. Do you want to go out next weekend?"

His lips curved up in a smile. "Yeah. I want to go out with you any night you'll have me."

"Next Friday night, then."

"I'm already looking forward to it." He pulled my hand up to his mouth and kissed it.

I went inside my apartment and closed the door, leaning my back against it and smiling. I was tired, but too excited to sleep. Being this happy was scary, but I also felt so incredibly good that I was sure the scary part was worth it.

FIFTEEN

REED

I WAS STILL IN high spirits from my date with Ivy when I went to my parents' house for a family dinner Sunday night. Other than the date, I'd done nothing but work and play basketball this weekend.

"Ribs?" I said, inhaling the smoky barbeque scent in the kitchen as soon as I walked in the back door.

Mom was standing over the stove, and she nodded and reached for me with a one-armed hug, stirring something on the stove with her other hand.

"It'll be ready in two minutes," she said.

"You need some help?"

"You can take that casserole into the dining room. But be careful, it's hot."

I picked up the dish with two towels and carried it to the large oak dining table, where Austin and Mason were sitting with Dad.

"Where's Hannah?" I asked Austin. "And Alana?"

"At a baby shower."

Mom walked in, carrying a huge platter of ribs. We all sat down and started passing dishes around. My stomach rumbled with anticipation. I hadn't eaten since breakfast.

"Kyle and Kim couldn't be here?" Austin asked.

"No," Mom said. "Kyle's working."

"What about Kim and the boys?"

"I invited them."

After a few beats of awkward silence, Mason spoke. "And . . . ? What's her excuse this time?"

Mom gave him a sharp look. "She never responded to my message. And no negative comments about family members."

"Really?" Mason's tone was aggravated.

"Really." Mom gave him another look and then passed me a basket of rolls.

"Mom, I actually think this is something we need to talk about," I said. "I'm concerned for Jordan and Eric, and I'm sure you guys are, too."

Dad cleared his throat and met my eyes across the table. "Of course we're concerned. But your mother and I decided before Kyle got married that we wouldn't interfere in our sons' families."

"I respect that," I said. "But this is . . . things have escalated recently. I heard Kim tried to pick up the boys from school when she was drunk. Is that true?"

"We don't know that," Mom said. "The rumor mill in Lovely is quite active, Reed. You of all people know that."

I nodded and sighed, about to try a different approach when Mason cut in.

"Just because people are saying it, doesn't mean it's made up. What if it is true?"

"If it's true, Kyle has a tough situation on his hands," Dad said. "But he hasn't come to us about it, so we're staying out of it."

"Kyle's got his head buried in the sand," I said. "He works so much he can't have much of an idea about what's happening at home."

"We don't disparage family members in this house," Mom said in a tone I remembered from childhood.

"It's not disparaging if it's true, Mom. He seems to have checked out of his relationship with Kim and, from what I've heard, someone should at least talk to him about it. He'd be more inclined to listen to you or Dad."

"You might understand better if you were married," Mom said softly. "That's the most important relationship in Kyle's life now."

Mason's exhale was full of aggravation, which matched the way I was feeling.

"Look, I couldn't give a shit about their marriage," I said. "That's not the point. It's Jordan and Eric. What if she's driven drunk with them before? Is she taking care of them?"

"She seems to spend all her time, and all Kyle's money, on jewelry and clothes and tanning," Mason interjected. "I never see her do anything for the boys."

"That is *enough,*" Mom said, sliding her chair back from the table. "You boys are grown men now, capable of making your own decisions, even if some of them are mistakes."

"This is bullshit," Mason muttered.

"Watch your mouth," Dad warned.

"Austin, back us up on this," Mason said.

Austin shook his head. "I think Mom's right about you guys understanding this better if you were married. If they get in between Kyle and Kim, they'd end up in a really awkward situation."

"Awkward is a hell of a lot better than the boys being in a dangerous situation, if you ask me." I tossed my napkin on my plate, my appetite suddenly gone.

"You'll appreciate our approach when you're on the receiving end," Dad said to me. "You won't hear anything negative in this house about your choices. If a waitress who's a single mom is your choice, we'll support that."

"Just what the hell is that supposed to mean?" I demanded angrily.

"It means you make your choices, not us. We support you whatever you decide."

"Well, I don't like your insinuation that Ivy being a waitress and a single mom is a bad thing. She works hard to support her son, which is more than I can say for Kim or Hannah." I looked at Austin. "No offense, man. And Ivy's a great mom. Noah's a hell of a lot better off than Jordan and Eric."

"I think we all need to take a step back," Mom said, putting her hands out in a gesture of peace.

"I'll step way back," I said, getting up from my seat. "I'm leaving."

The room was silent as I walked out. It was unlike me to argue with anyone in my family, but Dad's comment about Ivy had my defenses firing.

Things with me and Ivy were just getting started, but I knew she was someone special. Someone I wanted to stand up for. I'd never felt this way about a woman, and I wasn't letting her slip away for any reason. She deserved the same respect Kim and Hannah got from my family—if not more.

Dad walked into my office at work the next morning. "Got a minute?" he asked.

"Yeah."

"I want to apologize for my comment about Ivy last night. It was rude and uncalled for."

"Apology accepted."

He sighed and put his hands in his pockets. "And about Kyle . . . your mother and I never expected anything like this to come up. We *are* concerned about the boys. But it's tough when your sons are grown men, able to make their own decisions and mistakes."

I took off my reading glasses and set them on my desk. "It's not my place to question your parenting. I apologize for that."

Dad shrugged. "No need, son. We're all just doing the best we can. It means a lot to me that you care enough about Kyle and the boys to speak up."

After a few seconds of silence, he turned toward the door. "Lena's headed out to get some fancy coffee," he said. I smiled at his description of any coffee other than grocery store grounds brewed in the twenty-year old office coffee pot. "You want some?"

"Yeah, that'd be great. Thanks."

I buried myself in work that day and every one after that, catching up on public defender cases. I saw Ivy when I went to Gene's for lunch and we exchanged a few texts. But those bits of interaction just made me hungry for more. Every morning in the shower I fantasized about the sweet berry taste of her mouth when I'd kissed her, and the feel of her body pressed against mine. It always ended in a hard climax that barely satisfied my urge for her.

By Friday night, I was dying for time alone with her. She'd told me she was taking Noah to Margie and Gene's for the night, so I was picking her up there for our date.

When I knocked on the door of the neat little

bungalow, Gene answered it. He wore his trademark gray t-shirt, jeans and baseball hat.

"Reed," he said, reaching out to shake my hand. "You gonna take good care of our girl tonight?"

"Yes, sir."

"Come on in."

The house smelled like chocolate chip cookies. I followed the sound of Noah's laughter into the kitchen. He was standing on a chair in front of the kitchen counter, his hands covered with cookie dough.

"Hey, Noah," I said. "You making me some cookies?"

"Reed," he said, trying to stir the thick dough. "I make cookies."

"I see. They smell really good."

Ivy walked into the kitchen, her hands in the air as she pulled her hair up into a ponytail and wrapped an elastic band around it.

"Hey," she said, smiling.

"Hi." I wanted to kiss her, but it didn't seem right with Noah watching. She wore black cotton pants that fit her lean legs just right. I got a quick look at her hips and a sliver of her bare stomach as she tied her hair back. When she dropped her hands, her white t-shirt covered her again.

"Where are we going?" she asked. "Why am I dressed like this?"

"Fancy steakhouse," I said. "I always wear sweats to those places."

She approached and gave me a mock punch to the shoulder. "Seriously, why did you tell me to wear workout clothes?"

"It's a surprise."

"I don't like surprises."

I arched my brows and gave her a knowing smile. "You said that last time, and look how that turned out."

Her blue eyes were locked on mine and a smile played on her pink lips. I told my cock to keep his shit under control so I didn't get a hard on for Ivy in Margie and Gene's kitchen.

"You kids have fun," Margie said. "And Ivy, we're not expecting you back here tonight. We'll take Noah to the diner for pancakes tomorrow and then to run errands with us. We won't be back 'til afternoon."

I suppressed a smile. It sounded like Margie was encouraging Ivy to spend the night with me.

"Alright," Ivy said. "Thanks so much."

She approached Noah and turned him around on the chair, picking him up in a hug. "I love you," she said, squeezing him against her. "Be good, lovebug."

"He's always good," Margie said. "Noah's an angel."

"No eating raw cookie dough," Ivy said, setting her son back down on the chair.

"Oh, that's half the fun," Margie said, waving a hand.

"He shouldn't eat raw eggs."

"Bah. I ate worse than that when I was a kid. I was drinking beer at age fifteen," Margie added.

"Well, humor me," Ivy said. "Feed him all the cookies you want, as long as they're cooked."

"You got it. Now you two go on, get out of here."

Margie handed Ivy her gym bag and shooed us out the door. Ivy looked up at me as we walked to my truck.

"Where are we going?"

"Anyone ever tell you you've got a really cute belly button?" I asked.

She gave me a surprised look.

"I saw it when you were pulling your hair up."

"Oh." Her cheeks reddened.

"You know, you've got an innocence about you that's incredibly sexy," I said, backing her against the door of my pickup truck. "You blush over me seeing your stomach. What if I told you what I really want?"

"Are you . . ." Her cheeks darkened another shade. "Do you like to . . . talk dirty?"

"Not on the second date."

"But do you like it?"

My cock was hard, and it was all I could do not to press my hips against her so she'd feel it. But we were in Gene and Margie's driveway, so I maintained the inch of distance between us.

"I like *you*. And something tells me that, yeah, I'd enjoy talking dirty to you if the time was right."

She bit her lower lip before speaking. "I've never . . . done that, but something tells me I'd enjoy it, too."

I forced myself to step back. "Let's finish this conversation in the truck."

As I opened her door, I tried to come up with a thought that wasn't sexy. I had to get rid of this boner. Thinking fast, I pictured my mom and my grandma sitting at church. It helped. By the time I stepped into the truck, my sweats weren't tented anymore.

"You know," I said, turning to look out the back windshield as I put the truck in reverse, "you don't seem all that experienced, sexually."

"That's because I'm not."

"I find that very sexy."

Ivy laughed lightly. "My inexperience? What's sexy about me not having a clue?"

"I guess it's a guy thing," I said, shrugging.

"Hmm."

"Would you be turned off if I was inexperienced?"

"The thought hasn't even crossed my mind."

I cringed inside for being so forward so soon. "I apologize, Ivy. I'm moving way too fast here, suggesting that you've considered sex with me when we're on our second date."

She laughed again. "Oh, I've definitely considered *that*. What I meant was that I haven't considered you being inexperienced."

I let out an exhale of relief. "Well, I really like you a lot and I'm not in a hurry to get you into bed. I want you, but I want to do this right and let things happen like they should."

"And how is that?"

The truth slipped out of my mouth unchecked. "I want you to be in love with me first."

She was silent, and when I glanced over I couldn't read the look on her face.

"Did I say something wrong?" I asked.

"No. I'm just . . . That was really nice. What you just said."

Her tone wasn't just flattered, but surprised. I couldn't understand how this woman didn't realize any man would be a lucky bastard to have her fall in love with him.

"So, when the time comes . . . you *are* experienced, right?" she asked.

"Yeah."

"How experienced?"

"Enough. No worries, Ivy."

"I'm not as much worried as curious," she said. "How many women have you been with?"

Well, shit. I'd started this line of conversation and

now I was backed into a corner. I decided to try the dodge and deflect technique I'd learned in law school.

"What about you?" I asked.

When I chanced a glance at her, her face had crumpled. "Just one," she said, her voice nearly a whisper.

Something about the admission had been painfully difficult for her, but she'd done it. I wanted to be honest with her in return.

"I've been with eleven women," I said. "But when I was younger, sex was something different to me than it is now."

"How many of them were you in love with?"

"Just one."

She nodded.

"It's different with you, Ivy, I swear it is. I only want to make love to you, and I've never wanted that before."

"Me either," she said, her voice small.

I pulled into the parking lot of the gym. "We're here. Now let me put the smile back on your face. I'll be right around to get your door."

I took her hand to help her down to the ground and kept hold of it as we walked into the Lovely YMCA. I'd been coming here since I was a kid, and the front desk clerk nodded me past the front desk.

When we walked into the weight room, the heads of all dozen men inside turned to Ivy. I had a momentary urge to throw her over my shoulder and pound on my chest to stake my claim.

"What are we doing here, Reed? Tell me we aren't lifting weights." She turned to me with a small smile.

"I'm gonna teach you how to box," I said, leading the way to a punching bag in the corner.

"Really?" Her smile widened. "That sounds like fun."

We started with the bag, where I showed her proper form. There was nothing proper about the way I felt when I put my hands on her waist, or stood behind her to guide her arm the right way. I had to make sure I stood far back enough that she wouldn't feel the wood this was giving me.

Once she had the hang of it, I laced her hands into gloves so she could practice on me. We used the mat in the weight room, and I still noticed men staring openly at Ivy. She was too beautiful not to draw attention.

"Is that right?" she asked, punching the open palm I was holding in front of her.

"Elbow down a little," I said, easing it closer to her body. "Good, that's better."

Ivy was intent, working up a sweat quickly. The fiery determination in her eyes made me want to scrap the boxing lesson and make out with her instead.

"My arms feel heavy," she said after nearly an hour, stopping to rest.

"This is a real workout and I think we should call it quits. I'm planning dinner at my place, are you ready to go?"

She nodded and grinned. "But I love boxing. I want to do it again."

"We will. You want to shower here or at my place?"

Her horrified glance came as a surprise.

"I'm not trying to get you to shower with me on the second date," I said, raising my hands in surrender. "I didn't mean it like that."

"No, I was thinking about the open showers in the locker room here. I can't shower there."

"My place then."

I drove the short distance to my apartment above the

law office. When we walked in, Ivy looked around my loft apartment, her eyes drawn up to the exposed beams and tall windows overlooking downtown Lovely. It wasn't big, but the hardwood floors and gourmet kitchen made it just right for me.

"This is such a nice place," she said, sliding out of her coat.

"Thanks. I'll show you where the bathroom is."

But before I could, Snoop came bounding out of the bedroom, tail wagging. He went right to Ivy, his tongue hanging out happily as she petted him.

"Aw, you must be Snoop," she said. "You're a good boy."

He was as taken with her as I was. She gave his ears a good scratching before he walked away satisfied. After I led her to the bathroom and left her to shower, he laid outside the bathroom door, waiting for her.

I turned on some music and got started on the steak, mashed potatoes and asparagus I was making for dinner.

I was so absorbed in cooking that I didn't see Ivy come into the kitchen. A warm coconut scent made me look up from the counter and I realized it was her soap.

"You smell really damn good," I said, bending to kiss her neck. My hands were messy from peeling potatoes so I was forced to keep them to myself.

"I'll finish this while you get a shower," she said.

"You don't like a sweaty guy kissing your neck while he's making you dinner?"

I felt the vibrations of a low laugh in her throat. "I like it very much. I just figured you wanted to take a shower."

"I should." I wiped my hands off on the dishtowel I'd left on the counter. "Be careful, this knife's really sharp."

"I work at a diner," she said, her eyes sparkling with

amusement. "Don't you worry about me."

I couldn't stop grinning as I walked to the bathroom, pulling my t-shirt off and tossing it to the floor. When I turned the water on, it was already hot from Ivy's shower. I lathered my hair and body, rinsing off when I heard a dull pounding sound.

"Reed!" Ivy called through the door. She was knocking at the same time and her voice sounded panicked. I switched off the water, grabbed my towel and wrapped it around my waist. As soon as I threw the door open, I saw Ivy holding a red stained paper towel around one of her fingers.

"Oh, shit," I said in a rush. "Come here."

I grabbed a towel from the sink and wrapped it around her bleeding thumb. There was so much blood I couldn't even see the cut.

"You okay?" I asked. "Lightheaded?"

She shook her head. "It hurts, but I'm okay. It just won't stop bleeding."

"I'll keep pressure on it."

I squeezed both of my hands around the towel and raised her hand up in the air.

"I think we're supposed to keep the wound higher than your heart," I said. "I remember something like that from first aid training."

I hadn't dried off before opening the door, and now my wet chest was soaking through to her breasts. I stepped back to keep from getting her wet and felt the towel around my waist start to slide.

"Shit," I muttered. "Can you grab my towel? It's falling off."

She gasped and reached for my hip with her free hand. "This side? I can't see past our arms."

"No, other side."

I backed against the sink to hold the towel up. Ivy grabbed one corner and held it in front of me. We were a tangled mess of arms and wet body parts.

Both of us were silently avoiding eye contact until Ivy giggled and broke the tension.

"Only I, the queen of all klutzes, could pull this one off," she said.

"If you wanted to see the goods, you could've just told me. You didn't need to cut yourself to get in here."

"Funny."

"Have you got my towel?"

"As long as you don't move."

I lowered her hand and unwrapped it, able to see the gash in her thumb. Blood started to pour out of the cut again, so I wrapped the towel tightly around it again.

"You hold onto your towel for a few seconds so I can fix mine," I said. "Then we'll go into the kitchen and I'll wrap this cut up with gauze and bandages."

"I bled on the potatoes," she said apologetically.

"That's okay. I'm part vampire." I lowered her hand and met her eyes. "You ready?"

She nodded and I let go of her towel. I reached for the one around my waist and secured it tightly in a couple of seconds.

"Alright," I said, returning my hand to her towel. "To the kitchen."

I put my other hand on her back and led her there, where I washed the cut, dried it and put antibiotic on it before wrapping it with a thick layer of gauze, then securing it with tape.

"Tell me if it bleeds through, okay?" I said. "Just relax and let me finish dinner."

She watched me finish peeling the potatoes and add them to the boiling water on the stove, still wearing nothing but the towel around my waist. I'd sautéed the asparagus and put the steaks under the broiler before she finally spoke.

"You aren't the kind of person who says I told you so."

I made a face. "The world's got enough of those people, don't you think?"

"I do. But still, thanks."

"I'm gonna go throw some clothes on," I said. "We'll be eating in ten minutes."

I put on boxers, jeans and a t-shirt and ran a towel over my hair to dry it. When I got back to the kitchen, Ivy was leaning against the counter. Her bandaged thumb and expression of measured happiness made her look vulnerable. I wanted her to feel completely safe with me, but it I knew would take time.

"Hungry?" I asked, filling two glasses with water.

"Yes. Boxing works up an appetite. I had fun, though. I'd love to do it again."

"Anytime."

We sat down to eat and even though I was starving, I watched Ivy, waiting for her to taste the first bite. I was eager to see if she liked it.

She held the fork awkwardly due to her heavily-bandaged thumb. After a couple unsuccessful attempts to gracefully get a bite of potatoes to her mouth, she set the fork down and sighed.

"Want some help?" I asked, trying not to smile.

"Can you make me left-handed?"

"No, but I can feed you."

Her cheeks flushed. "That's okay, it'll just take me a

little longer."

She ate slowly and we talked about work and Noah while we sat there. After we were done, I stacked the dishes in the sink, saving them for later.

Ivy was playing with Snoop, but she stood up from scratching his back when I approached. I cupped her cheeks in my hands and went in for the kiss I'd been waiting for all week.

She kissed me back, her tongue brushing across mine. Her sweet coconut smell made it hard to hold back. I wanted more of her. When I kissed her deeper and she gripped my back, I wondered if I'd ever be able to get enough.

I slid my hand from the back of her neck under the collar of her t-shirt to her shoulder, wrapping my palm around the slight lines of it. She moaned softly and I ran my other hand up past the bottom of her shirt to the warm skin of her waistline.

Ivy had never been touched by a man in the right way. I could tell by the way she jumped slightly before melting into me every time my hands wandered someplace new. I wanted to lay her down on my bed and spend hours slowly exploring every inch of her. Her sighs and moans made my cock ache for more.

It was too soon for us to sleep together, so I couldn't take her into my bedroom. I walked her over to the couch and put my hand on her back, easing her onto it. The glimpse I caught of her from above took my breath away. Her cheeks were pink and her chest rose and fell as she looked at me, arousal pooling in her bright blue eyes.

I'd wanted her since the moment I saw her, and I finally gave in to the primal urge she brought out of me. I took her hands and put them on the armrest of the couch, holding them as I laid on top of her and kissed the soft skin of her neck.

Her body stiffened beneath mine.

"No, Reed," she said, sounding panicked. "Stop. *Please.*"

I scrambled off her in a rush, my head swimming with confusion. "What's wrong? Are you okay?"

She stood and wrapped her arms around herself. "I don't know." She straightened out her clothes and smoothed a hand over her hair. "No. I'm not okay."

"Shit, I'm sorry. I thought—"

"It's not you," she said, her eyes dark with sadness. "You didn't do anything wrong. I've been *not okay* for a while now. Since before I even met you."

Her gaze darted around the apartment like she was looking for something.

"Was it me being on top of you? Is that what upset you?"

"Where's my purse?" She went to the kitchen in search of it.

"Ivy." I followed her. "Are you leaving?"

"I need to go."

Her eyes had a frantic look now, like a trapped animal desperate to escape.

"Did someone hurt you?" I wanted to walk the few steps separating us and take her in my arms, but I forced myself to stay rooted in place. I didn't want to scare her again.

"Where's my purse?"

Tears glistened in her eyes and I felt a surge of emotions. Seeing her hurt made me feel helpless. Knowing I'd scared her made me feel like an epic asshole. And realizing someone had given her a reason to fear men this way filled me with a rage that ran hot in my veins.

"It's on the table in the living room," I said.

She practically ran there, grabbing her purse and the sweatshirt she'd left next to it. Within a second, she was out the door, her feet pounding down the stairs in a rush.

I wanted to follow her. It was all I could do not to run after her and tell her I'd drive her home. I didn't want her to be alone while she was so upset, but she needed to escape, and I had to respect that. She needed to escape *me,* which hurt like hell.

The terror in her voice when she'd told me to stop replayed in my mind over and over. The night had gone from one of the best I'd ever had to one of the worst in a matter of minutes.

SIXTEEN

Ivy

AFTER LEAVING REED'S APARTMENT in a panic, I'd practically run over to Margie and Gene's. I'd only gotten a few nosy questions from Margie about my date with Reed before I said good night and went to curl up in bed with Noah.

She knew something was wrong, which was why she didn't press me. After we left Margie and Gene's Saturday morning, Noah and I spent the rest of the weekend playing trains and cleaning the apartment. And I spent a lot of time thinking about what had happened on Friday night.

Going back to work Monday morning was good for me. The hustle and bustle of the diner kept my mind off things with Reed.

Margie and I stood together behind the counter at the diner, her stocking a pie case and me starting a fresh pot of coffee. I groaned when two brunette customers walked in and sat down at one of my tables.

"What?" Margie asked.

"Those two at Table Twelve. They're complete bitches to me every time they come in and they always tip me a penny."

Margie turned to look and then gave a 'hmm' of recognition. "Well, no wonder. You know who that taller one is, don't you?"

"No."

"That's Julie Marsh. Tom Marsh's wife."

"Great," I muttered. "She probably blames me for him getting suspended from his job."

"She ought to blame *him*." Margie stacked her tray with plates of food. "I'll take Table Twelve."

"No, it's fine."

"You sure?"

"Yeah, but thanks."

I considered making them wait, but decided to get this over with instead. The brunettes were both glaring at me when I approached their table.

"Can I start you off with some drinks?"

"I dropped something, can you get it for me?" Julie Marsh asked, eyes wide and innocent.

I bent to look under the table. "There's nothing but a used Kleenex under there."

"That's it. Get that for me, will you?"

I stood upright and shook my head. "Sorry, no. Can I get you guys some drinks?"

"You're my server, aren't you?" Julie asked in a nasty tone.

"Unfortunately, yes."

"So serve me."

I laughed. "My duties stop at serving the food you order. Look, I have other customers. Would you like drinks or not?"

"I'd like to talk to your manager."

"Margie? Sure. She's the one who told your husband not to come back in here. She'll be glad to talk to you."

I turned to get Margie, stopping after just a couple steps when I heard Julie say a single word.

"Slut."

"Excuse me?" I faced her.

"You heard me. I said you're a slut."

I eyed her trashy outfit and bit back a comment.

"We have kids, you know." She narrowed her eyes at me. "And my husband's gonna lose his job because of the scene you made. Don't prance around in here shaking your ass if you don't want men to look at it."

"Your husband did more than look."

She stood up and pointed at me, her face reddening with anger. "You're a whore. Stay away from my husband."

Something inside me snapped. Being called a whore and a slut when I was pregnant had cut me deep. I'd left that shame behind, and being labeled those things in Lovely was more than I could stand.

I grabbed an empty plate from a vacant table and held it high, throwing it to the floor with all my strength. It shattered into bits against the tile, silencing the diner.

"I am *not* a whore!" I yelled at Julie. "You don't even know me. How dare you call me that?"

Margie was behind me, wrapping an arm around my shoulders.

"You two need to go," she said to Julie and her friend. "Don't come back."

All eyes in the diner were on me as Margie led me into the kitchen. Once we were safely there, I broke down in Margie's arms.

"I'm so sorry," I said tearfully.

"No apology needed, Ivy. I know how stressed out this whole thing with Tom has you. Julie had no right coming in here and treating you that way."

My body sagged weakly against hers. It wasn't Tom that was upsetting me. It was the way I'd treated Reed the other night and the anger I still felt over the letter from my father.

Gene put a hand on my back. "Why don't you take the rest of the day off, Ivy?"

"No," I pulled away from Margie and wiped my palms over my face to dry it. "I'm okay."

"Take a few hours for yourself," Margie said. "We've got things covered."

"Would it be okay if I work back here for the rest of my shift? I can rotate stock and get the dishes done. I could use a break from customers."

"Of course," Margie said. "But you need to eat some lunch first."

"I need to go clean up that plate."

"Shawn's got it." Margie smiled and left to go back to the floor. We were full. I wondered if Reed would come in today.

"What can I make you to eat?" Gene asked.

"I'll make a salad. Thanks, Gene."

"Here." He plated a piece of grilled chicken off the grill. "Put some protein on it."

The savory smell of the freshly cooked chicken made my stomach growl. I took it and went to the prep table to make a salad.

I was a hot mess and I didn't know how to make things better. After lunch I lost myself in a mountain of dishes, wishing the hot soapy water would wash away my worries.

"Ivy?" Margie called behind me. "It's after two, honey. You're off."

"Oh. I'm almost done."

"Someone brought you something."

I turned around, my wet hands dripping onto the tile floor. Margie held a dozen fresh red roses in a milk jug with the top cut off.

"Reed." Tears welled in my eyes.

"Did that boy's mother not teach him what a proper vase looks like?"

I laughed and approached Margie to smell the fragrant flowers. "It's kind of an inside joke. Oh, Margie, he really is so sweet."

"You found a good one."

"Is he still out there?"

"He's at the counter waiting on lunch."

I dried my hands on my apron. "Do I look okay?"

"Beautiful as always," Margie said. "I'll set these flowers on my desk for you to take home when you go."

I nodded, already halfway to the double doors connecting the kitchen to the dining room. When I pushed them open, I saw Reed at the counter, wearing a navy blue suit. His face was unshaven—just the way I liked it.

He turned as I approached, sliding off the stool he was sitting on.

"Thank you," I said, reaching up to cup his cheeks in my hands. "I'm kind of soaked with dishwater right now or I'd hug you."

He bent and wrapped his arms around me, pulling me into a hug so tight he lifted my feet a couple inches off the floor.

My tension faded away in the warmth of his arms. "I'm sorry about the other night," I whispered in his ear.

"Don't be. I want to respect your boundaries, but I need to know what they are."

"Sometimes I don't even know."

Reed pulled back, rubbing his hands down my upper arms. "We'll figure it out together, Ivy."

I nodded, my heart full of gratitude for this man who accepted me with open arms—quirks, fears and all.

"Can I take you and Noah to Jimmy's for dinner this week?" he asked. "And another date for the two of us whenever you're ready?"

"Yes."

I didn't know if I was capable of having a physical relationship with a man. But after getting a taste of one with Reed, I knew what I was missing. I'd gone to sleep with an ache between my legs every night since our failed second date. My head told me to stop this and go back to the safety of my isolated existence, focusing all my energy on Noah.

But my heart craved more of the closeness we'd shared. Even after my freak out, Reed still wanted me. If he accepted me as I was, maybe it was time I accepted myself that way, too.

JIMMY'S ITALIAN PLACE WAS crowded, and I was pretty sure at least half the people here were speculating about me, Reed and Noah sitting together in a booth.

"Do you feel like people are looking at us?" I asked Reed.

"Yeah. You know how it is in a small town like this."

"I'm hungry," Noah said, looking up at me from our side of the booth. "Want some scapetti."

I ruffled his hair, smiling at his mispronunciation of spaghetti. "It'll be here soon, sweetie. Want some bread and butter?"

He nodded solemnly and I reached for the basket of bread in the center of our table.

"I want Reed to do it," Noah said. I looked at him, my brows lowered with surprise.

"Sure thing," Reed said, reaching for a piece of bread. "Do you like lots of butter or a little bit?"

"Lots of butter," Noah said, smiling.

I sat back, watching the two of them. Since my son was born, I'd never felt the need to bring a man into our lives. I'd never questioned whether I was enough, because I knew I was. I loved Noah with everything in me.

And now I realized it wasn't about *needing* a man in our lives. Reed was here because I wanted him here, and because he deserved to be. Being around my son was a privilege I'd never cared to extend to any man. It felt good, having someone with us who cared enough to ask if Noah wanted a little butter or a lot.

Reed turned over his placemat and drew Noah a train, complete with a waving conductor in the front. He was no artist, but Noah's eyes lit up as he pointed out the wheels and the caboose.

My heart was full. This moment felt too perfect to be real. I didn't even feel self-conscious as I slid my hand across the table and slipped it into Reed's. His eyes met mine as he stroked a thumb over my knuckles.

"Will you guys come to my parents' house for Christmas dinner?" he asked.

"Oh." I tucked my hair behind my ear as I considered.

"We always do Christmas morning at Margie and Gene's. We open presents and then go into the diner to make the meal we serve free for people who don't have a place to be that day."

"We do a family trip to church on Christmas Eve and a family dinner on the evening of Christmas Day," he said. "What if you guys do those things with me and I'll come help make the meal at the diner on Christmas morning?"

"You might get stuck peeling potatoes."

"I don't mind."

"Okay. It sounds awesome."

After that evening, Reed started spending more time with me and Noah. We'd make dinner at his apartment, where Noah and Snoop would chase each other tirelessly. One weekend we drove to St. Louis and took Noah on a train ride.

And when Christmas morning came, he did get stuck peeling potatoes at the diner. I snuck peeks at him from the other side of the diner's kitchen, where I was helping Noah mix pumpkin pie batter.

"Wonder what you're smiling about?" Margie said with a knowing smirk.

"I can't help it," I admitted. Wearing jeans, a worn red flannel and a Red Sox baseball hat, Reed was a poster boy for rugged sex appeal. I loved the way his scruffy cheeks felt against my neck when he kissed me there.

We'd backed things up physically since that night when I'd left his apartment in a panic. Now we only kissed, though just that was often enough to get me hot and bothered after a few minutes.

"You two are the talk of the town, you know," Margie said. "There were already whispers, but when everyone saw you sitting together at church last night, with Noah in his lap . . ."

Reed looked up from his work on the other side of the room and smiled at me.

"Good things happen to good people," Margie said. "I'm happy for you, Ivy. I just hope you'll still have time for me and Gene."

I turned to her, my brow furrowed. "Of course I will."

She sighed softly and put the finishing touches on a fluted pie crust. "The Lockharts are a big, close-knit family. If you become one of them—"

"Margie." I laughed softly. "That's not happening anytime soon. Reed and I haven't even–" I glanced at Noah, "*you know.*"

"But if it does happen—"

I put my hand on her arm. "If it does happen, it won't change anything between us. You and Gene are family to me and Noah. We love you guys."

"We love you, too," Margie said, tears shining in her eyes. "Gene and I were never able to have kids, and you're the daughter and grandson we always wanted. Keeping Noah on Friday nights . . . it's not a chore. It's the highlight of our week."

"It's the highlight of his, too." We both looked at him, stirring the pumpkin pie puree with an intent look on his face. "You know, when I came here, I was completely alone. And now Noah and I are lucky enough to have you guys *and* Reed in our lives. We need all of you."

Margie smiled. "I'm so relieved to hear that." The doors between the kitchen and the lobby were pushed open and she glanced into the crowded room of Lovely residents.

"Did you see who's out there?" she asked.

"Looks like half of Lovely. We've got more people than last year. I love how festive everyone is."

"Walter Grieves is here. That's a first."

"Walter?"

"You should go say hello to him."

I reached for a towel and dried off my hands. "I'm going to."

We had Christmas music playing in the restaurant, but it was being drowned out by the sounds of conversation and laughter. This wasn't just a meal for people who couldn't afford to make a traditional Christmas dinner, but it was for anyone in Lovely who didn't have another place to be.

Walter was perched on his usual stool, a paperback in his hands. I made my way over to him and tapped him on the shoulder.

"Merry Christmas," I said when he turned.

"Ivy." He smiled. "You're looking well."

"Better than two days ago?" It was the last time I'd served him breakfast, since Margie had given me Christmas Eve off.

"Just in general, I suppose. You look happy."

"I am happy. And I'm really glad you're here."

He shrugged. "It's not Christmas without turkey, right?"

"True. It's also not Christmas without the people you care about, so you're in the right place."

A moment of awkward silence passed.

"I need to get back to the kitchen," I said, waving a hand at the double doors.

"Of course. I need to get back to this story." He smiled and tapped his paperback.

"I was actually going to ask how your potato peeling

skills are."

"Mine?"

"Yeah. Reed could use some help, and I'm pretty sure he won't let me near a knife after the way I cut myself last time I peeled potatoes at his place."

"Can't say I blame him." Walter looked at me over the lenses of his glasses. "I'd be glad to help."

He closed his book, grabbed his coat and followed me into the kitchen.

We were so busy with the meal that we only had time for a few quick bites of food ourselves. By the time Reed, Noah and I got to his parents' house that evening, we were all starving.

Grace had prepared an elaborate, traditional meal. The whole family was there—even Justin, the youngest of the brothers.

The family gift exchange after dinner was like nothing I'd ever seen. With so many people, presents were stacked high around the tall Christmas tree in the family room.

Noah's gleeful squeal when he opened the train set Reed got him brought tears to my eyes. Margie and Gene had also bought him one to keep at their house, which he'd opened this morning.

What little extra money I had, I'd spent on Noah for Christmas. But I'd managed to buy Reed a scarf, which he put on as soon as he opened it.

"I love it," he said, kissing me in front of his whole family. Noah kissed me immediately after, apparently feeling like it was the thing to do.

When I opened my gift from Reed, my breath caught in my throat.

"A laptop?" My mouth dropped open with shock.

"Reed, this is too much."

"No, it's . . . just say you love it."

"I *do* love it, but—"

"Good. You need it for your school work, and now you can email your friend April without having to go to the library. I got you Internet service, too."

"Ivy," Grace asked, "You're taking classes?"

I nodded. "It'll take me forever, but I decided to start working on an English degree."

"That's wonderful. I'm so proud of you."

"So am I," Reed's father Henry said. "Good for you, Ivy."

Henry had never spoken to me, and I could tell he was trying to make a start.

"Thank you," I said. "My friend Walter kind of inspired me to do it."

We stayed at Reed's parents' house til almost midnight. Noah was playing with the other kids and I was getting to know the rest of his family. Even when my mom was alive, I'd never been around a big family. It felt good to be with the Lockharts.

Noah fell asleep on the way home and Reed carried him inside and put him to bed. I was yawning in the living room when he walked out of the bedroom.

"I'll go so you can get to bed," he said.

I approached him and wrapped my arms around his waist. "Can you stay for a little bit?" I asked softly. "We haven't had any time alone today."

"Yeah, I can stay a little longer. Mason went to my place to let Snoop out earlier."

I snuggled against his chest, resting my cheek on the soft fabric of his flannel. "You smell like potatoes," I said.

"You smell like pumpkin pie. It's kinda sexy."

I laughed and untucked the back of his shirt, running my hands up over his bare skin. He pulled me tightly against him and I looked up at his face.

"You know what I've noticed?" he said, brushing his thumb over my jaw line.

"Mmm?" I said, closing my eyes and moaning softly as he gently cupped the back of my neck.

"You like it when I touch you. It doesn't matter where it is." My eyes fluttered open as he traced the pad of his thumb across my lips. "You like me touching you slowly and gently, especially if we're standing or you're on top of me. The only thing that ruins it is if you feel overpowered by me."

I gazed up at him, his coffee-colored eyes seeming to see inside me.

"True?" he asked softly.

"Yes."

"Has a man ever forced himself on you?"

I kept my eyes locked on his, my mind warring with itself. I'd decided to tell him when his thumb brushed over my lips again. It felt so good that I kept my lips pressed closed as he outlined my upper lip and then my lower one.

"You don't have to answer. I know from how scared you were that night I laid on top of you. That tore me up, Ivy–knowing I made you feel that way. I'd never hurt you. I couldn't."

I nodded slightly, leaning closer so I could feel the warmth of his chest against mine.

"You have to talk to me, okay?" he said. "I need to know what you like and don't like. What triggers bad memories, so I don't do it. I can't let go when we're together if I'm worried about scaring you."

"It's like you said . . . if I feel overpowered or trapped, it's hard for me. I do love it when you touch me. No one's ever touched me like you do. When you go really slowly . . . it does things to me."

"Does it, now? Tell me more."

"I like it when you touch my back. When you run your finger down my spine. And when you put your hands under my shirt to rub my shoulders."

"I can't wait to see all of you," he said, his thumb tracing my jaw line.

"I want to try," I said tentatively. "As long as you know I might freak out again. It might not work."

"Try . . . ?"

"Sex. I want to. With you."

He pushed his brows together, looking concerned. "Are you sure?"

"Completely sure. As long as you get that I'm very inexperienced, and I can't stand feeling trapped."

"I'll go slow. But . . . I wanted to wait until—"

I put a finger over his lips, silencing him. "I do, Reed. But I want to wait until that night to say it. Do you?"

"I do. Very much."

Warmth radiated to every nerve ending in my body. "Okay. So we're going to try. When?"

He considered. "This weekend? I want to make some plans, and I'll need a couple days."

I bit my lip, trying not to laugh over his rock-hard erection against my stomach.

"What's funny?" he asked.

"I can, um . . . tell you approve of this idea."

"Hell yes, I approve." He pulled both my hands up to his lips and kissed them. "I promise to make it good for you, Ivy."

I smiled, forcing away the twinge of apprehension churning in my stomach. Reed didn't realize what he was dealing with. I felt guilty for not telling him, but I wanted this to happen without him thinking of me as a victim. I just wanted to be a woman making love to a man for the first time. Maybe it wasn't possible for it to be good for me, but I wanted to try. For Reed, but mostly for myself.

SEVENTEEN

MY STOMACH WAS IN knots as I waited for Reed to arrive. The day was finally here. We were going away for our first night together. I'd dropped Noah off at Margie and Gene's and told Margie to wish me luck.

She hugged me and did just that, though she probably thought she was wishing me luck on a simple date.

I'd packed a bag of things and splurged on a small bottle of perfume. The anticipation was killing me. After several sleepless nights in a row, I was hoping to fall asleep curled up next to Reed later tonight. Much, much later tonight.

When he pulled up in front of my apartment, I stepped out, locked the door and ran out to his truck, my bag and purse in hand.

"Hey," he said, smiling when I opened the passenger door and got in. "You eager tonight?"

"A little. Aren't you?"

"A lot." He leaned in for a kiss. I relished his coffee and chocolate taste for a few long seconds before leaning back and reaching for my seat belt.

"Where are we going?" I asked.

"It's a surprise."

I groaned, but couldn't keep myself from smiling. He'd taken the time to plan something special, and that reminded me that he was worth facing my fears for.

"You want to listen to my Sex playlist?" he asked.

I gaped at him. "You have a Sex playlist?"

"I made it this afternoon. I was in court at the time, actually, waiting for my hearing."

"Way to multitask. So these are songs that put you in the mood?"

"Songs that remind me of you." He pushed a couple buttons on the dashboard of his truck and 'I Want You' by Kings of Leon came on.

"I like it," I said, leaning back in my seat to listen to the music.

When we went through the outskirts of Lovely but he just kept driving, I gave him a puzzled look.

"There's nothing for almost an hour this way. Unless you're taking me to the gas station in that next little town."

"I'm not. We'll save that idea for next time, though." He turned next to a sign for the Lovely Airport.

"Are we going to the airport?" I looked at him, hoping for a clue. "It's not a real airport, is it?"

He laughed. "No commercial flights or anything, but it's real."

"Hmm."

The rural airport was all runways and big metal storage buildings. Reed parked next to one and my stomach started churning.

"Tell me you don't have an airplane," I said just before he closed his door. He jogged around to my side and opened my door, offering me a hand.

I took his hand and stepped out, looking at him expectantly. "Tell me, Reed. Because there is no way—"

He pressed a finger to my lips, silencing me. "I don't have a plane."

I breathed out a sigh of relief.

"But my dad does," he said, winking at me. He led me by the hand to the door of the building we'd parked beside.

"Wait," I cried, digging my feet into the ground. "I can't go on a plane."

"Sure you can."

"No, I can't."

He looked at me, waiting for an explanation.

"I mean . . . I've *never* been on a plane," I said. "I'm afraid of flying."

"I've been flying for a decade. I promise you I know what I'm doing."

"It's . . . not you," I sputtered. "It's the plane."

"We'll only be in the air for thirty minutes." Reed looked down at me, his dark brown eyes imploring me. "Please, Ivy. I'd never put you in danger."

"This is why I live in a bubble," I muttered. "There's so much I've never done. I'm not like other women, Reed."

"And I like that about you." He squeezed my hand. "Listen, if you really don't want to go, we'll drive."

Something in his tone tugged at my heart. "No. I'll go. Just please don't kill me."

He shook his head and gave me a sideways smile. I let him seatbelt me in and put my headphones on, and I concentrated on the reason we were doing all of this. He got on a radio and talked to someone and I squeezed my eyes shut.

The plane started moving and I gripped the sides of my leather seat with both hands, not opening my eyes until Reed had eased the plane from the ground to the air. Everything beneath us was getting smaller. I couldn't deny that this was exciting and maybe even a little bit fun.

I smiled over at Reed and his expression relaxed.

"Okay?" he asked. I nodded, taking in Lovely from the air through the plane's windshield.

The plane was small but the ride was smooth. Reed's face was lined with concentration as he lowered the plane slowly and landed it on a runway in an otherwise vacant field.

"Where are we?" I asked as he helped me step down.

"This place belongs to some friends of my parents. It's their vacation place."

A path led us through a clearing and about a quarter-mile of forest. When we emerged, I sucked in a breath as I saw the building in front of us.

It was a sprawling log home, larger than any I'd ever seen. Built on a lake, it had a spectacular view of the water. There were dozens of windows and the wide front door was flanked with potted pine trees.

"Wow," I said under my breath. "It's amazing, Reed."

"Yeah, they're loaded."

"Said the guy whose parents have an airplane." I smiled at him.

The corners of his lips quirked up. "My favorite part of this place is over this way."

He took my hand and led me around to the water. I pulled my coat closed with my free hand to block out the chilly winter wind.

"Almost there," he said.

When we stepped onto a wood dock, I looked down and saw that both sides were lined with small floating candles in glass bowls of water.

"Reed, this is so—"

I was silenced when I saw the wood gazebo at the end of the dock. Candles glowed from atop a table inside. Reed led the way down the dock and opened the gazebo door.

The sweet scent of fresh flowers filled the air inside. A table for two was set, complete with a vase of white hydrangeas.

"We're having dinner here?" I asked, shedding my coat and looking out at the sparkling water surrounding us.

"Yes. The caterers are working in the house, but they'll serve it out here."

"This is so beautiful, Reed," I said as he pulled out my chair for me. "It's . . . beautiful here. And it's warm. How is it warm in here when it's winter?"

Reed smiled and sat down across from me. "It's heated. If it was summer, I'd row us out on the water to watch the sunset."

"Sounds amazing. Have you ever done that before?"

"Just once with my Mom."

The sound of footsteps on the dock made us both turn. A middle-aged man dressed in black was approaching, and he opened the gazebo door.

"Mr. Lockhart?"

"Yeah, that's me." Reed stood and walked over to shake the man's hand.

"I'm Antonio, and I'll be serving your dinner. May I start you with some wine?"

"Sure. Ivy?"

He looked at me and I shook my head. "Just some ice water would be great."

Antonio nodded and departed.

"You look nervous," Reed said.

"I am," I admitted.

"We don't have to do this if you're not ready."

I squeezed my hands together under the table. It wasn't that I didn't feel ready. I knew there was a world of difference between what my father had done to me and what Reed and I had been stopping short of doing for a couple months now. Everything Reed did made me feel good. More than good. I felt treasured. Sexy. Desirable. And the way my body responded to his was better than I'd ever thought possible. With him, I wanted it all. I just worried about how my subconscious would react.

"I'm ready," I said. "As long as we go slow, I think I'll be okay."

Our drinks came, and I tasted Reed's red wine. Surprisingly, I liked it, and he gave me an amused grin as he took the bottle from the wine coaster on the table and refilled the glass.

"Sorry," I said, sliding the glass across the table.

"Keep it." He slid it back. "I'm glad you like it. I can drink out of the bottle, either that or Antonio can bring us another glass."

Antonio brought in a salad and bread, followed shortly by a baked pasta dish, and our conversation slowed as we ate. By the time we finished with cheesecake and fresh berries, the sun had set and the glowing candles were the only light in the gazebo. We talked and laughed until the moon was bright in the sky.

"I'm feeling so relaxed now," I said, sitting back in my seat. "Like *super* relaxed."

Reed's eyes were warm and a smile danced on his lips. "It's the wine."

"Well then, wine for the win. I needed a little something to loosen me up."

He reached for my hand and I leaned forward and twined my fingers into his.

"Ivy." His face was serious now. "I want you to know that I love you. I love you in a way that's more full and certain than I knew love could be. Every day with you is better than the last."

I reached my other hand across the table and wrapped both of mine around his big one. "I love you, too. You've brought me out of myself and I can't remember why I ever thought I didn't need you. You make me feel things and want things I never thought I'd want."

"You ready to go inside?"

I took a deep breath and nodded. We walked the short distance to the main house, a stunning log home with vaulted ceilings and a huge wall of windows overlooking the lake. The moon was bright tonight, its reflection shimmering in the water.

We'd just tossed our coats onto a chair when Reed approached me and cupped my cheeks in his hands. He looked at me intently for a few seconds before kissing me softly.

I parted my lips, eager for the warm brush of his tongue against mine. We kissed each other deeply, neither of us able to get enough. Our hands roamed over and under clothing until Reed pulled back, leaving me staring at him breathlessly.

"You want to move to the couch?" he asked, his eyes dark and hungry.

"I was thinking the bedroom."

He nodded and led the way up an open staircase to a cozy bedroom with a king-sized bed covered with a rustic quilt. The room was intimate, not open and enormous like the main level.

"This room is nice," I said.

Reed's expression was intense as he cupped my jaw gently. "Tell me you'll say so if I need to stop."

I nodded.

"You have to talk to me, Ivy. Tell me what you like and don't like. We're learning as we go here–both of us."

Warm excitement coursed through me. I walked over to the bed and sat down. Reed followed me and sat next to me. He brushed the hair back from my face and kissed me, his hand sliding from my chest around to my shoulder.

I laid back, grabbing two fistfuls of his flannel to pull him down with me. But he stayed frozen in place several feet above me.

Confused, I lowered my brows and was about to ask him what was up when he wrapped his hands around my hips, picking me up as he laid down and then set me on top of him.

"That was an impressive move," I said, grinning.

"You need to be on top."

His expression was filled with reverence as he looked up at me. He wanted this to be good for me, but he didn't feel sorry for me. I marveled at his ability to still make me feel sexy when he couldn't even be on top of me.

"Reed Lockhart," I said softly, reaching for the top button on his flannel. "I love you so much."

He closed his eyes as I unbuttoned his shirt and pushed it open. When I laid down on him and felt his hardness against me, I moaned and pressed my hips against his.

I kissed him and he slid his hands up my back, pulling my shirt up and then off over my head. My black satin bra was simple. But his gaze made me forget it was from the Walmart Clearance rack. I felt like the sexiest, most powerful woman in the world.

His hands moved slowly and deliciously over every inch of my skin. When he unclasped my bra and circled his thumbs on my nipples, his touch feather-light, I sat up and arched my back.

The friction of him against my core was sending waves of warm pleasure to every one of my nerve endings. I pressed his hands against my breasts, a cry escaping my lips when he squeezed them gently.

"Oh, God," I said, my voice hoarse. "More."

He wrapped his arms around my back and sat up, flicking his tongue over one of my nipples. He gently squeezed one breast while licking and sucking the nipple of the other. My mouth hung open in an unending gasp and I wound my fingers into his hair.

By the time he finally unbuttoned my jeans, I was so desperate for more of him that I stood up and wiggled out of them. His small smile sent a wave of confidence through me. That, and the erection straining against his jeans, which was *not* small.

Climbing onto the bed between his legs, I unbuttoned the fly of his jeans. He groaned when my fingers brushed over his erection, so I pulled his jeans down enough to stroke it more thoroughly.

"Ivy," he said in a low, strained voice. "Shit . . . that's good."

I felt his legs tense beside me. When I gripped the waistband of his jeans to pull them down, I didn't realize

I had his boxers, too. His erection sprang straight up into the air and I gasped, both impressed and horrified.

When I climbed back up to straddle him this time, he wrapped his palms around my ass, pulling me against him.

"Lay on your back for me," he said. I leaned down and kissed him before sliding off his lap and doing as he asked.

This time he was the one climbing onto the foot of the bed. He kneeled there and picked up one of my legs, setting it on his shoulder. For a few seconds, he just looked at me as he slowly ran his hand from my ankle to my thigh.

"Remember what I said about talking to me?" he said.

"It feels good," I said, the words coming out in a gasp. "So good, Reed."

His eyes darkened as his mouth moved to the side of my foot, which he kissed gently. The brush of his stubble against the delicate skin there made me jump at the same time I moaned.

"Oh, God," I said, panting. "Good. It's good."

He kissed his way to my ankle, and I closed my eyes, taking in the sensations coursing through me. When I felt a soft brush against the fabric of my panties between my legs, my eyes flew open and my back arched off the bed.

"Wet," Reed said, sounding satisfied.

I wanted to ask him to touch me there again, but instead I gripped two fistfuls of the quilt on the bed as his lips trailed up my calf to my knee, which he kissed for what felt like a full minute.

My body was on fire by the time he made it to my inner thigh. I was writhing on the bed, not caring how shameless and out of control I looked. I *was* out of control, and it was sublime.

Reed hooked his fingers around my panties and pulled them down excruciatingly slowly, his lips following the decent of my panties down my thighs.

"*Damn*, Ivy," he muttered, staring between my legs. "You're so much more beautiful than you were in my fantasies."

I tried to close my legs, self-conscious about the reddish curls his eyes were fixed on. But he held my knees, not allowing me to hide myself from him.

"I can . . . shave," I said softly. "I should have."

He shook his head. "You're perfect. And really fucking hot. Don't shave."

When he picked up my foot and kissed my ankle again, I cried out with exasperation.

"Something wrong?" he asked, amused awareness in his tone.

"No . . . I don't know. I just want more."

"More what?"

"I want you to touch me," I said, sounding desperate.

"Where?"

"Reed . . . you know."

I gathered my confidence and moved a hand between my legs, running a finger down my seam. "Here."

His lips parted as he watched me. When he kissed his way up my thigh this time, he wasn't so gentle. My back arched off the bed when I felt his warm breath between my legs.

I was expecting his fingers, so the warmth of his mouth on me made me cry out loudly.

"Reed! I don't know if I can take that."

He scooped his hands beneath my hips and held them in place. When his tongue touched me, I thought

193

I might explode from the deep wave of sensation that swept through me.

Words eluded me. I just gasped and panted as his tongue explored me. The pleasure built, and I was close to climaxing. I'd wanted to wait for sex, but this was too good to stop.

I was seconds away when he stopped and I groaned with frustration.

"I'll finish you that way later," he said, kissing my stomach. "I promise."

He reached for his jeans on the floor, fishing a condom out of a pocket. I watched him rip it open with his teeth and roll it on, his silhouette dim but distinguishable in the darkness.

My body was humming with arousal. It was hard to remember what I was afraid of in this moment. Reed laid down on his back and put his hands around my hips, guiding me on top of him.

"It's all you, baby," he said in a low tone. "Take as much of me as you want."

"I don't know . . . how to do this."

"Just relax." He laid a hand on my stomach and ran it up to my breasts, cupping them one at a time.

He wrapped his other hands around my hip, and the feel of his hands on my skin incited me again. I lowered myself toward him and he guided me to the right spot with his hand on my hip.

The brush of him against my opening made me gasp with pleasure, but as I slowly sank onto him, my gasp turned into a sharp inhale. I stopped, taking a second to adjust to the fullness of him inside me.

"Fuck," he mumbled in a strained tone. "You feel so damn good, Ivy."

I lowered myself a little more and he gripped my hip tightly before releasing me and reaching for the wrought iron rails on the headboard. With a ragged exhale, he grabbed two rails, his body tense beneath me.

"Is this okay?" I asked tentatively.

"It's incredible. I can't keep from taking control unless I put my hands here. Don't stop."

I rocked my hips, moving myself up and down slowly at first, and then at a steady, more confident pace.

Reed groaned every time I sank onto him. Knowing my body turned him on aroused me as much as the sex did.

I moaned loudly as the hot ache inside me built, moving faster.

"Grab the headboard," Reed said, his voice strained. "Let go of your inhibitions, baby. You feel so fucking good."

I reached for the top rail of the headboard and wrapped my hands around it, bracing myself so I could ride him harder and faster.

From his groans, I was sure Reed was in exquisite pain as he held on to his orgasm. My own started taking over and I cried out his name and gripped the rail.

"I love you so much, Ivy," he said, sitting up and wrapping a hand around my shoulder. He pulled my hips down against his as we came together in a mix of frantic cries and groans.

I collapsed onto my side, panting hard.

"Jesus," Reed said, blowing out a breath. "That was fucking amazing."

"It was. I didn't know it would feel like that."

He wrapped his arms around me and pulled me close. "I wasn't sure you'd be able to come the first time.

That was so hot."

"That was my first orgasm that wasn't from touching myself," I admitted.

Reed kissed me, slow and soft. "First of many."

In high school, I'd been naïve enough to think I was in love with Levi. But this deep, all-encompassing fullness in my heart was true love. I was feeling it for the first time with Reed, and I hoped it would last.

Our weekend passed in a haze of lovemaking, amazing food and wine. On the flight home, I rested my hand on Reed's thigh and stared out the window. Our time together had been dreamlike, but I was looking forward to getting home to Noah.

I was content for the first time I could remember. It was a delicious, full feeling. I'd known Reed was worth opening up for, but this was beyond anything I'd hoped for. Love had a magic all its own and I wanted to live under this spell forever.

EIGHTEEN

I PUSHED OPEN THE diner's back door, breathing hard. The familiar smells of bacon grease and coffee greeted me as I grabbed my apron from its hook and put it on while running across the kitchen.

As soon as I walked from the kitchen to the floor, I scanned the room and found Margie. She was taking orders at the counter so I stood to the side and waited for her to finish.

"Sorry I'm late," I said.

"It's fine. Everything okay?"

"We couldn't find one of Noah's shoes. We searched the whole apartment and I was about to take him to daycare in socks and flip flops when I found it in one of the kitchen drawers."

"What a rascal," Margie said, grinning.

"Yeah, he was pretty amused. I think he'd forgotten about hiding it in the drawer because he seemed as surprised as me when I found it." I looked around the crowded dining room. "I'll take my usual tables."

Margie nodded toward the kitchen. "Got a second?"

197

"Sure." I followed her through the doors and she gave me a concerned look. We were alone except for Gene, who was absorbed in cooking on his wide grill.

"Everyone's kind of in shock," Margie said. "Chuck Ashley was arrested yesterday evening. Charged with raping his stepdaughter Chloe. She's sixteen. Apparently he was videotaping it, so the evidence is solid."

My stomach dropped to the floor. "That's terrible," I said, hoping Margie wouldn't see just how deeply the news was upsetting me.

"Yeah. Chuck's our banker. He's on the school board. I never would've thought someone like him was capable of this."

I laughed humorlessly. "Margie, you can't judge something like this based on those things. There are hidden monsters all over the place."

"It's an awful shame. Things like this don't happen much in Lovely."

"Does the girl have anyone there for her?"

Margie nodded. "From what I heard, her mother didn't know what was going on and she's shocked, but trying to support her daughter."

"That's good."

Squaring her shoulders, Margie looked out the windows in the double doors that separated the kitchen and dining room. "We need to get back out there. I just wanted you to know what the talk's about this morning."

The diner was abuzz with the news. At every table, the conversation was about Chuck and his stepdaughter. Some people claimed they weren't surprised, others commented on the low-cut dress Chloe had worn to a recent dance and another group said Chuck would burn in hell for what he'd done.

Every conversation grated on my nerves. If the allegations were true, this girl's life had been changed forever. It wasn't right for strangers to be discussing her violation over coffee and eggs.

But if I'd learned anything in my twenty two years, it was that the world had plenty of people who couldn't care less about what was right.

REED'S SECRETARY LENA NODDED at me as I walked past her desk. She was always cordial, but I sensed her disappointment every time I came by the office to see Reed, probably because she was the sister of his ex.

I bypassed her without a second thought today. Reed knew I was coming because I'd texted him when I left work. I needed the comfort of his presence right now.

When I walked into his office at the end of the hallway, he looked up from his desk, taking off his dark-rimmed reading glasses.

"Hey, Beauty," he said, smiling as he got up to meet me halfway across the room.

I pushed the door closed and threw myself into his arms. His warm, musky cologne was becoming a familiar scent to me. I pressed my face against his chest and breathed it in.

"You okay?" he asked softly.

"I just needed this. It's been kind of a lousy day."

He kissed my temple, holding me tightly against his chest. "Missed you at lunch. I had an eleven-thirty meeting and court at one."

"It's better seeing you alone anyway," I said, pulling back so I could look up into his eyes. "Do you have a few minutes?"

"Of course. We can sit if you want. But first . . ." He cupped my cheek and kissed me. "Okay, now we can sit."

I took one of the leather club chairs in front of his desk and he took the other, turning his chair so we were knee to knee.

"Have you heard about Chuck Ashley?" I gripped the arms of my chair nervously.

"Yeah."

Reed's brief answer gave me an opening to continue. This was my chance to tell him why the news about Chuck had struck me so deeply. I was ready for him to see the darkest parts of me.

"I've been upset about it since I heard this morning," I said. "His poor stepdaughter. I just—"

Reed put a hand on my knee, an apology in his eyes. "Ivy, I'm sorry, but I shouldn't discuss any aspect of this case with you or anyone else."

I felt a flutter in my chest. "What?"

"I was assigned to defend Mr. Ashley at the one o-clock call today."

My lips parted with shock.

"It's gonna make me unpopular around town, I know," Reed continued. "If anyone gives you any shit over it, you tell me. I'm just doing my job, but not everyone sees it that way in a small town."

"A rapist?" My voice was barely audible. "You're defending a rapist?"

His brow furrowed. "Alleged. And yes, I am. Bart, the main public defender, has a conflict because he represented Mr. Ashley in another case before becoming the PD."

My head spun with dizziness even though I was

sitting. "But . . . so your job is to discredit his stepdaugh-ter, then? Call her character into question? Make her out to be a liar?"

He leaned forward and rested his palm on my thigh. "I haven't even opened the file yet. Ivy, what's going on with you? You're worrying me."

"You asked before if someone had hurt me." My voice broke and I cleared my throat before continuing. "Well, someone did."

Reed closed his eyes, his shoulders dropping forward in defeat. "Dammit, Ivy. I didn't want it to be true. I'm so sorry."

He hung his head for a few seconds and when he looked up at me, tears glistened in his eyes. "Do you feel ready to talk to me about it?"

"I did," I said, wrapping my arms around myself. "But . . . I can't do it now. You're defending a rapist. I'm on one side of this, and you're on the other side."

When Reed sat back in his chair, the hurt in his eyes tugged at me for just a second. But no. He wasn't hurting anywhere near as much as me.

"This is my job, Ivy," he said. "I don't advocate sexual assault any more than I advocate drunk driving or parole violation or any of the other things I defend people for."

Nervous energy propelled me up from the chair. "When he goes on trial, you'll be sitting next to him. You'll plan a way to get him off."

He sighed and ran a hand through his hair, clearly aggravated. "I don't even know if it'll go to trial. It's still very early."

"How can you sleep at night, knowing you could be helping a rapist do something so horrible again?" My voice shook and the tears I'd been holding back spilled over.

"That's an oversimplification of my job, sweetheart." Reed rose and approached, trying to wrap me in his arms again.

I backed away. "Not now."

"I love you. You've just shared something painful about your past with me and I need to be there for you right now. Don't let this case come between us."

"I can't help it. You don't understand."

"I want to understand, though. Help me understand."

I closed my eyes, my heart threatening to pound its way out of my chest. "I wasn't ready to tell you everything, Reed. Just that my heart has been broken all morning for that girl because I was raped, too. You probably already realized it, from when we talked before. It's how I got pregnant with Noah."

Reed's face crumpled. "I'm so sorry."

"Don't say that," I said fiercely. "Don't ever say that. He's the best thing that ever happened to me."

"I didn't mean it like that. I'm just sorry about the whole goddamned thing, Ivy. I can't imagine how painful it must've been."

"No, you can't. You're a man. And you'll be defending another man who stole things from that girl that she can never get back."

"How can I make this better? I get why you're upset with me. But I don't get to choose my cases."

"Can't you just turn this one down?"

He shook his head. "It doesn't work like that."

"I can't be here anymore," I said, clutching my purse to my side and stepping toward the door.

"Please don't go."

"I was already upset, and now . . . I can hardly hold it

together. And I have to go get Noah."

"Ivy." Reed's tone was pleading. "Stay. Talk to me. Be with me. Don't walk out like this."

My hand was on the door handle when I turned to look back at him. "I can't be with a man who would defend a rapist. I know it's probably not normal to feel this way, but . . . I just can't."

Reed's eyes were wide with shock. "Don't do this. I love you. I love Noah. We can work this out. Just please don't walk out that door."

I turned the handle and stepped out, wiping the tears from my cheeks. Leaving his office was just a formality. In my heart, I was already gone.

SEVERAL WEEKS PASSED. AT first I felt like I was surrounded by a fog, carrying a cloud of sadness around me everywhere I went. It didn't help that Noah asked to see Reed and Snoop every day.

I thought about calling him so many times. Sometimes I even sat on my couch after Noah was in bed, just staring at the screen of my phone and reading the many text messages he'd sent me since I'd left his office that day. I knew I'd overreacted. But the problem was, I didn't know any other way to be anymore.

Freaking out when Reed was on top of me was also an overreaction, but it came from a subconscious place in me I had no control over. Those horrible minutes in my bedroom four years ago had changed me. Now I was a woman who felt a deep connection to others who were violated, and a deep disgust for any man who'd done it.

I picked Noah up from daycare one day, wondering

in the back of my mind if April had responded to my recent email. Though I had planned to return the laptop to Reed, I still had it for now. When I got home and opened the computer, I saw that she'd responded, but it wasn't the sort of message I'd expected.

Hello Ivy. My heart is heavy after reading you've broken up with Reed over the case he's been assigned. As a friend, I'm here to support you, but I also have to say I think you've made a huge mistake.

It's time to be honest with yourself. You took this girl's sexual assault so hard because you, too, were assaulted and you still haven't completely dealt with it. I was proud of you for going to counseling when you first got to Lovely, but it sounds like when the counselor pressed you to open up about what happened, you stopped going to sessions.

What happened changed the course of your life. But, at some point, you have to realize that you're in control now. You get to decide if you seek help or stay buried under the weight of what happened.

Reed is a good guy, Ivy. From everything you've told me about him, I know he's serious about you and Noah. Stop sabotaging your own life and forcing yourself to be alone. Reed is doing his job, and nothing more. Talk to him. I know it's hard, but be brave. You deserve happiness.

Much love,
April

I sat back, reading the message three times before signing out of my email. April was right. I'd pushed away the best thing to happen to me since Noah. But I knew in my heart that if I went to Reed and apologized, it would be hollow. I'd still feel the same pain and resentment about him defending Chuck Ashley.

After I picked Noah up, we ran errands and then went back to the diner for dinner. Gene was sick with the flu and Margie was taking care of him so they'd asked me to keep an eye on things in their absence.

I carried Noah into the kitchen and made a sweep through it. The second shift cook, Nick, nodded at me. He had the place looking as good as Gene would have. I wiped down the prep table out of habit and took Noah back to the lobby to eat.

"Where's Gene and Margie?" he asked, used to seeing them here every time we came in.

"They're at their house," I said. "What sounds good for dinner?"

"Go to Gene and Margie's." He grinned at me.

"We would, honey, but Gene's sick. Do you want a cheeseburger?"

He nodded and we settled into a booth, where he asked me to draw a picture of a train. I did my best, but he frowned at me.

"Where's Reed?" he asked.

I sighed and set down the purple crayon I'd been drawing with. "He's probably at his office, buddy."

"Want to see Reed." Noah tried to slide out of the booth.

"No, we can't." My heart tugged in my chest. "Want to dump out the sugar packets?"

He grinned and slid back into his side of the booth. Dumping out the sugar and putting the packets back in the container one at a time was one of the ways he kept busy when he was here.

I watched him with half an eye as I looked over at

the two boys sitting together at a table in the corner. They were familiar to me. I waited for their parents to return from the bathroom or wherever they'd gone so I could place who the boys were, but after fifteen minutes, they still sat alone.

"Noah, let's walk over here for a bit," I said, taking his hand to help him down from his seat.

We were on the way to check on the dark-haired boys when it hit me. They were Jordan and Eric Lockhart, Kyle's sons.

"Jordan and Eric, right?" I said, approaching the table with Noah.

The older boy, Jordan, nodded. They'd pushed their dirty dinner dishes off to the side to make room for two boxes, which they were decorating with markers.

"Are your parents here?" I asked.

"Our mom's picking us up later," Jordan said.

"Did she drop you off here for dinner?"

Jordan nodded. "And to make our Valentine's boxes."

A surge of concern laced with anger passed through me. "How old are you guys?"

"I'm seven and my brother's five," Jordan said.

"You know what?" I said, lifting Noah into one of the empty seats at their table. "I know your Uncle Reed, so how about if I call him and he can come here and we'll help you decorate these boxes?"

"Okay," both boys said, smiling.

"Will you ask him to bring some tape?" Jordan said, pulling out a broken flap on his box.

"Sure."

I grabbed my phone from my purse and dialed Reed, who answered on the second ring.

"Ivy. God, I miss you. I'm so glad you called. Why haven't you answered any of my messages?"

After an awkward moment of silence, I said, "I'm at the diner. Jordan and Eric are here. Kim dropped them off and they ate alone and now they're decorating their Valentine's boxes here."

"Jordan and Eric?" Reed's tone was incredulous. "My nephews?"

"Yes. They're too young to be here alone."

"I'll be right there. Stay with them, okay?"

"Of course."

I asked a waitress I knew well to sit with the kids while I went to Margie's office to get some tape. I'd just started helping Jordan tape up his box when Reed walked in the front door, his chest rising and falling from breathing hard.

My own breath was trapped in my throat. I hadn't seen him in weeks, and it was all I could do not to jump up from my chair and run into his arms. He hadn't come in for lunch since our argument.

His eyes never left mine as he approached the table.

"Hey," he said.

The second he noticed Reed, Noah jumped down from his chair and threw his arms around him in a hug. Reed bent down and picked him up, and the sight of my son in his arms almost brought me to tears.

"Where Snoop is?" Noah asked.

"He's at home taking a nap," Reed answered. "How are you, Noah?"

"Good. I want to color."

Reed put him back in his seat and Noah started coloring the box I'd found him in the kitchen. Doing what the older boys were doing seemed to make him happy.

"Hey, guys," Reed said to Jordan and Eric. "What are you doing here by yourselves?"

"Mom dropped us off," Jordan said. "She'll be back later."

"Where was she going?" I heard the disguised unhappiness in Reed's tone.

Jordan shrugged.

"Where's your dad?"

"Working."

Reed nodded. "Okay. You guys want some help with these boxes?"

"Yeah!" Eric said. "Can you make mine into a spaceship?"

"I'll see what I can do," Reed said, pulling up a chair.

His chair was next to mine, and though we weren't touching, I could feel the warmth of his leg next to mine. I was close enough to catch a hint of the woodsy cologne I remembered smelling on his skin. My body responded to his presence, all my nerve endings coming to life at once, though my expression gave nothing away.

"Thanks for calling me," he said to me in a low tone.

"Were you still working?" He wore jeans, work boots and a flannel, but he also had on the dark-rimmed reading glasses I'd only ever seen him wear at his office.

"Yeah, doing research. I was working from my apartment, though."

"If you haven't eaten, I can get you something."

After a moment of silence, he leaned toward me and whispered in my ear. "I miss you so damn much. I love you, Ivy."

His words and the warmth of his breath on my skin made me feel like a puddle of hormones on the floor. I wanted him. Wanted it all. It was all I could do not to crawl into his lap and tell him I felt the same way.

"Mama, where's my cheeseburger?" Noah asked, breaking the spell I was under.

"Um . . ." I took a deep breath to clear my head. "I'll go check on it. Reed, you want anything?"

"I'm good, thanks."

When I got back to the table with Noah's plate, Reed stood up.

"I'm gonna run over to the drugstore and get what we need to finish these boxes," he said. "And I need to call Kyle."

I nodded, avoiding his gaze.

"Hey," he said softly. "Walk me to the door."

I followed behind him and he turned to me when we were alone.

"Say something. I'm dying here, Ivy. Have been for more than a month now."

"I miss you, too," I acknowledged.

"Jury selection's starting tomorrow. The trial should start in three days or so. Do you think you might feel differently when it's over? Maybe we can move past this then?"

I shook my head helplessly. "I just don't know, Reed. I realize how wrong it is that I feel this way."

"It's not wrong that it upsets you. But it's wrong for you to think I'm ever on any side but yours. I'd do anything for you."

"I want to move past what happened to me, but—"

Reed's eyes darkened seriously. "I'm not asking you to move past it. I don't think a woman ever gets past that. I'm asking you to accept me as I am, public defender job and all. I accept you that way, Ivy. I want to be there for you and it fucking hurts when you push me away. What

I'm saying is that I'm yours, and now it's up to you to decide if you want me."

I closed my eyes for a second, willing myself not to cry. When I opened them, Reed had turned to the diner's door. He pushed it open and left, leaving me feeling lower than ever.

When Reed came back with the supplies for the boxes, we both helped the boys decorate them. Kyle came in just as we were finishing, wearing dark green scrubs.

"Dad!" Eric cried, sliding down from his chair. "Look at the spaceship Uncle Reed made me!"

"That looks great," Kyle said, smiling down at his son. He walked over to the table and looked back and forth between me and Reed.

"There were here all alone?" he asked in a low tone.

Reed nodded. "And they'd still be here alone if Ivy hadn't called me."

Kyle shook his head, his face lined with tension. "Thanks, Ivy. I really appreciate this. Do you know how long they were here before you called Reed?"

"I'm not sure. At least half an hour, because that's when I got here."

"Ivy," a waitress named Addison called from behind the counter. "Okay if I make the kids ice cream sundaes?"

All three boys cried out their excitement and rushed over to the counter.

"Sure," I said, knowing Noah had no idea what he was so excited about. He was just following the lead of the older boys, and it was cute.

"Hope that's okay," I said to Kyle.

He waved a hand dismissively. "Of course."

"Look, you can get pissed at me if you want," Reed said to Kyle. "But listen to me first. You need to confront

Kim about her parenting skills. This shit's got to stop."

Kyle rubbed a hand over his unshaven face. He looked tired, both physically and mentally. "Yeah, I know. Part of me wants to stay here with the kids to see how long it takes her to show up."

"And whether she'll be sober when she gets here," Reed said.

Kyle's face fell. "Yeah, that too."

Reed folded his arms across his chest. "Here's a better idea. I'll take the boys back to my place for the night. They can sleep in my bed and I'll take the couch. You wait here for Kim."

"Okay," Kyle said. "Thanks, little brother."

They gave each other a quick hug and I stepped back, feeling like I was intruding. While the boys finished their ice cream, Kyle sat and talked to them and Reed and I picked up the box decorating supplies.

We both reached for a marker at the same time, our hands touching. A current flowed from his warm skin into mine. He started to pull his hand away, but I grabbed it and held on. I couldn't look at him because I knew I'd cry.

After a few seconds, I let go and turned, swallowing the lump in my throat. I picked Noah up and said goodbye to everyone, still not able to make eye contact with Reed.

Life without him had been so much easier when I didn't know what I was missing.

NINETEEN

CHUCK ASHLEY'S TRIAL WAS a major event in Lovely. It seemed like everyone in town was either at the trial or talking about it. It had just started today, and already I was ready for it to be over.

Lunch rush at the diner had been so crazy that we hadn't even been able to seat everyone. Gene had somehow worked his magic and made carryout orders for those who wanted to eat but couldn't be seated.

The close proximity of the courthouse was the reason for our crowd. The courtroom couldn't seat everyone who wanted to watch the trial, and Gene's was the closest restaurant for people to grab a quick lunch and hurry back to secure their seats in the courtroom.

It was after one o' clock now, and the diner was practically empty. The trial had resumed a few minutes ago. Margie had gone over with the lunch crowd, hoping to get a seat.

I was sweeping the floor and wiping down tables, leaving the serving duties to another waitress so I could clean up without distractions. My mind was wandering today anyway.

The lunchtime chatter had been about the opening arguments of both attorneys. Apparently Mark Cameron, the state's attorney, had given a compelling open about Chuck grooming his stepdaughter to be his victim. Reed's open had been short and succinct, encouraging the jurors to keep an open mind and consider all the evidence.

My cell phone buzzed in my apron pocket and I pulled it out. Another voicemail from April. She'd left several over the past week and I'd never found time to call her back. I was almost done cleaning the lobby and I hadn't had a break all day, so I asked Gene to make me a grilled cheese and I took my phone out back, where I dialed April.

"You live," she said sarcastically.

"Sorry. It's been crazy."

"I figured you were avoiding me because you knew I was calling to ask about Reed."

"There's nothing to tell," I said, biting into my sandwich.

"Ivy, why are you pushing away a great guy?"

"It's not exactly easy to go from no relationship of any kind for four years to falling in love before I knew what hit me," I said. "Sorry if that came out snappy."

"Hang on while I find a tissue to wipe away my tears," April said. "You fell in love with a sweet, hot guy who loves you and Noah. You poor thing."

"You don't understand."

"Do you? Does this even make sense in your own head?"

"I don't know," I admitted. "He's in the middle of the trial right now, and I want to go watch it, but it's so hard to see him."

"Talk to him, for crying out loud."

"How are things with you?" I asked, hoping to change the subject.

"No complaints. I've got a date tonight."

"So the long distance thing didn't work out?"

"No, but it's for the best."

I stared at the sliver of the courthouse building I could see from the alley, wondering what Reed was doing right now.

"I have to get back to work," I said. "Thanks for calling. Really. Will you let me know how the date goes?"

"Sure. And you let me know how it goes when you talk to Reed."

I smiled. "Bye, April."

"Bye."

WHEN LUNCH RUSH ENDED the next day and Margie asked me if I wanted to try to get a seat at the trial, I surprised myself by saying yes. I wasn't sure if it was my secret desire to see Reed or the way I identified personally with the case, but I wanted to see for myself what everyone had been speculating about.

The courthouse was a grand old stone building with marble floors and staircases. The trial was on the third floor, so I followed the crowd and ended up in a huge courtroom with tall ceilings and rows of wood benches. It was ornate, with a mural depicting the scales of justice and a large, carved wood desk where the judge sat. Framed portraits of former judges lined one wall.

I slid into the end of one row near a portrait of a judge wearing a curly wig. Just as I took my seat, the modern-day judge rapped his gavel and called for quiet in the courtroom.

My gaze landed on Reed's broad back. His hair curled the tiniest bit near his collar and I thought longingly about how much I'd loved the feel of his hair between my fingers.

He sat straight in his chair, and I knew the man next to him had to be Chuck Ashley. All I could tell about him from this angle was that he had short blond hair.

The judge told the prosecuting attorney to call his next witness, and when he said Chloe Trenton's name, a collective murmur ran through the crowd.

"Quiet," the judge said sternly, rapping his gavel. "We will have order."

The room stilled as Chloe was led into the room through a side door by a bailiff. She kept her eyes down as she approached the bench and was sworn in as a witness.

She was a slight girl with dark hair and olive skin. Wearing dark dress slacks and a dark sweater, she looked like she wanted to avoid attention.

The prosecutor started with a series of routine questions about who Chloe was and how long she'd known her stepfather. Everyone listed in rapt silence. When the prosecutor asked her if Chuck was in the courtroom and asked her to identify him, she looked directly at the table where Reed sat and identified her stepfather by pointing at him.

It had started as mutual flirtation, she said solemnly. Then her stepfather begin touching her in non-sexual ways. A pat on the back, a hand on her arm. Then it grew into kissing with his hand up her shirt or down her pants.

"How did you react when this would happen,

Chloe?" the prosecutor asked, leaning against the wood rail of the jury box.

"I . . . liked it. I wanted it to happen." Her expression clouded with shame.

"How did the subject of sex come up for the first time?"

She sighed before continuing. "My mom was out of town for the weekend. Chuck kissed me and asked if I wanted to take things further between us."

"And what did you say?"

"I said yes."

Chuck leaned toward Reed and whispered something in his ear. Reed didn't move or acknowledge him, and Chuck moved back to his side of the table, clearly agitated.

"Can you describe what happened next?" the prosecuting attorney said.

"We went to my bedroom," she said, looking down at her lap as she spoke. "We kissed and Chuck took off my shirt and all of his clothes. Then he took off my pants and told me to lay down on the bed."

"What did you do?"

"I told him I wasn't sure I wanted to do it. I was scared, and it didn't feel right."

The prosecutor approached the stand and spoke to Chloe. "Can you tell the jury what exact words you said to him?"

"I said, 'I don't think I can do this.'"

"And what did he say in response?"

She sighed again. "He said, 'It's too late. I'll get blue balls if we don't do it now.'"

"What happened then?"

"He pushed me onto the bed and . . ." she paused to

compose herself, "pulled my underwear off."

A sick taste rose in my throat. This was all too familiar.

"What did you do and say, Chloe?"

"I said no. I kicked and tried to get away. But he held me down and . . . did it anyway."

"I know this is hard, Chloe," the prosecutor said, "but can you tell the jury what he did?"

"He had sex with me. He raped me."

"Did you realize that immediately?"

She shook her head. "He told me it was consensual since I led him on. But I said no. I said it so many times. So when my mom got home from her trip, I told her, and she took me to the police station."

When the prosecutor sat down at his table, the judge looked at Reed.

"Mr. Lockhart?"

"No questions, your honor," Reed said.

When Chloe stepped down from the stand, I could see that her hands were shaking. She clasped them together and they steadied.

I admired the grace of this young woman. Just sixteen years old, and she'd been brave enough to stand up in court and confront her stepfather. Brave enough to speak some hard truths.

Suddenly I felt a strong urge to do the same.

WHEN THE JUDGE CALLED a break in the trial, I walked back to the diner, still thinking about Chloe. I pushed the back door open and walked in, and Margie peeked at me through the pass through. As soon as she saw me, she came charging through the double doors into the kitchen.

"Something's wrong," she said. "What's wrong, Ivy?"

I took a deep breath and looked up to meet her eyes. "I need to go somewhere alone. It's a long drive, and I don't know if I'll be back tomorrow night or Sunday. Can you pick Noah up from his daycare and keep him for me?"

She hesitated before answering. "Of course. But I don't like the look on your face right now. I feel like something's wrong."

"I'm okay. This is just something I've needed to do for a while."

"I don't mean to pry," she said, the corners of her eyes creased with worry, "but does anyone know where you're going? I don't want you running off if no one has any idea where you're going."

"I'm going to my hometown. Lexington, Michigan. I have to see someone there."

"Someone dangerous?"

I laid a hand on Margie's arm. "It's a family member. Everything's okay, I promise."

"You'll have your phone with you? And you'll call us if you need to?"

"I will. Thanks for taking care of Noah."

Margie threw her arms around me in a hug. "Be careful."

"Don't worry about me."

I stopped at home and threw some clean clothes, my toothbrush and toothpaste into a bag. My heart was racing as I got into my car to start the long drive to Lexington. Just the thought of seeing the town again made me nervous. I couldn't imagine what seeing my father would do to me.

It was time, though. Past time. I wasn't going to let the past hold me back anymore.

With every hour of the drive that passed, my resolve grew stronger. As I crossed state lines, I found I was eager to confront the man I'd been hiding from. A switch had been flipped inside me, not just from losing Reed, but from watching Chloe face her stepfather and say out loud what he did to her.

By the time I pulled into Lexington and made the familiar trip to my childhood home, it was after midnight. I parked several driveways down from the one with my father's marked squad car in it, locked all my car doors and reclined my seat, hoping to get some sleep before seeing him for the first time in more than four years.

The sound of a car engine woke me up. I pulled the coat I'd covered myself with off of my face and squinted from the bright sunlight.

Sitting up, I ran a hand down my face and glanced out the window at the neighborhood I'd grown up in. Not much had changed.

It was Saturday, which I hoped meant my dad was off work. I checked the driveway in my rearview mirror and saw the squad car. A jolt of nervous anticipation hit.

Chloe had done it, and I could, too. I started my car and drove to the house, parking in front. Seeing the brick front steps where my mom had taken my picture on the first day of school every year brought on a sharp pang of longing for her.

I got out and approached the front door, taking a steadying breath before raising my hand and knocking.

A woman with long blonde hair opened the door. She wore a pink fuzzy bathrobe and carried a mug of coffee.

"Can I help you?" she asked, smiling.

"Is Brad here?" I cleared my throat, trying to process what I was seeing. Apparently Dad had moved on with this woman.

"Babe," she called behind her. "Someone here for you." She turned back to me. "Would you like to come in?"

I nodded and stepped into the living room. With new furniture, it didn't look like the house I'd grown up in. Pictures of a girl and a boy on one wall made my skin prickle nervously.

"Ivy?"

Dad stood in the doorway.

"Ivy?" The woman turned to me. "I'm so sorry. I should have . . . Come in, please. I'm Beth. It's so great to finally meet you."

I ignored her, my eyes locked with my dad's. His hair was grayer at the temples and he looked about ten pounds heavier. But otherwise, he looked the same as I remembered. Thanks to the nightmares, I was sure I'd never forget his face.

"Beth," he said, "can you—"

I interrupted before he could finish. "Who are the kids?" I nodded to the school pictures on the wall.

"They're mine," Beth said. "Ben and Cara."

"How old are they?"

She looked at me, apparently uncomfortable with my cold tone. "Um . . . eight and eleven."

I narrowed my eyes at my father. "And they live here? Those kids live here?"

After a few moments of uncomfortable silence, Beth spoke. "I'll leave you two to talk."

"No, you need to stay," I said, breaking away from my father's gaze to look at her. "Do your children live here?"

"They visit their father every other weekend. That's where they are now, actually, but they're with us the rest of the time."

I shook my head, anger welling inside me so strong it was all I could do not to cross the room and physically attack my father.

"How?" I asked bitterly. "How could you?"

He sighed and looked down. "Ivy, I needed to move on. I loved your mother—"

"Oh, I couldn't care less about that. I mean the kids. Does she know?"

His expression hardened. "Don't do this, Ivy."

"Know what?" Beth said, looking at him.

"I need to talk to my daughter alone," he said firmly. Beth started to walk away.

"No. You need to say," I said, my voice thick with emotion.

I looked at my dad again. "Either you tell her, or I will. Right now."

His expression twisted with disgust.

"Tell me what?" Beth said again, crossing her arms over her chest. "What's going on, Brad?"

"Ivy's got some issues," he said, transforming from pissed off to sympathetic in an instant. "She kind of lost it when her mother died."

"Are you kidding me?" I cried, angry tears welling in my eyes. "More like I kind of lost it when you raped me."

Beth stumbled and pressed a hand against the wall for support.

"You can't trust what she says," my father said, approaching her. "She doesn't know what she's saying."

Rage ran hot through my veins. I didn't want to be

capable of hatred, but he was testing my capacity.

"You're disgusting," I spat at him. "Not just for doing it, but for lying. Own it, *Dad*. You felt pretty big and bad that night, didn't you?"

There was contempt in his eyes when he looked at me. "What is it that you want, exactly, Ivy?"

"I came here to tell you that the part of me I thought you ruined is actually going to be okay. I won't spend one more day feeling different or disgusting. You're the disgusting one. And thank God I needed to say that. Otherwise, who'd have warned Beth who she and her children are living with?"

Dad turned to me and roared, "I am not a monster!"

"You are to me. You would be to my mother if she was still alive."

"How dare you . . ." He took a couple steps toward me and I forced my feet to stay in place.

"Brad," Beth said in a tiny voice. She looked like she'd had the wind knocked out of her. "Is this true?"

"No."

I scoffed at his emphatic denial and looked across the room at Beth. "He's lying. Your children aren't safe here."

"You know me, Beth," Dad said. "You know I'm not capable of such a thing."

Her expression softened.

"You don't have to take anyone's word for it," I said, my eyes leveled on my father. "A simple DNA test of my son will prove it."

Silence hung in the room until Beth's sob cut through the air.

"I don't know why you hate me so much," my dad said, sounding defeated. "All I ever wanted was to move on."

"Other than the fact that you raped me? How about the fact that my son will one day be horrified to find out who his biological father is? Or the fact that I still have nightmares about that night? Maybe the emotionally-crippled state it left me in? I have so many reasons to hate you, Dad, but you're just not worth it."

He sighed deeply and I noticed the lines on his face for the first time.

"You've taken what little I had, Ivy," he said sadly. "Anything else?"

"Yes. You either resign from your job in the next forty-eight hours or I'm seeking sexual assault charges against you."

His eyes darkened with anger. "You want to see me ruined, is that it? Want to make sure I've got nothing left?"

"You've got no right being in a position of authority." I walked to the door, putting my hand on it before turning back to him. "Resign or don't. It doesn't really matter because I need to move forward with charges anyway and you'll lose your job when you get convicted. If I don't do it, you might find another woman with kids."

"I'm not a sicko," he said, his voice tight with anger. "I was blackout drunk that night. It was a horrible mistake that I regret."

"And you'll have to live with the consequences," I said. "I'm done being too ashamed to admit what happened out loud."

I glanced at Beth one more time. She sat against the wall, her legs pulled up to her chest, her face blank with shock.

I didn't say goodbye. I just walked out the door knowing I'd never walk back through it. It wasn't home anymore, anyway. Everyone I loved was in Lovely, and I smiled as I thought about how proud every one of them would be if they could see me now.

TWENTY

AS I SPENT THE rest of my Saturday driving home, there was only one place I wanted to go. I needed to see Reed and ask him to forgive me. I craved the comfort of his strong arms, though I wondered if he'd open them to me after the way I'd behaved.

I hadn't treated him like a man I loved and trusted. He's treasured me, and I'd turned my back on him.

By the time I pulled in to a parking place behind his building, the sun had set. I took a deep breath and stepped out of my car. His truck was here, so I knew he was inside.

I climbed the outside steps to the second floor and knocked. When he opened the door, I resisted the urge to throw myself against him. He wore a navy t-shirt and jeans, his feet bare.

"Ivy," he said. "Come in." He stepped aside and I went in.

"Hi."

"Are you okay?"

"Reed . . . I miss you and I need you. I've been such

an ass. I'm sorry. Can you forgive me?"

He pushed the door closed in a swift motion and reached for me, pulling my feet from the floor as he held me tight.

"Yes. I've missed you so much it hurts."

He set me down and kissed me. My body responded to his in an instant, my curves molding against him as I parted my lips and moaned as his tongue found mine.

"Hold on," I said, pressing my palms against his chest. "I need to tell you something."

He looked down at me, his hands resting on my hips.

"This is the hardest thing I've ever done. But I have to. I want you to see all of me."

"What is it, Beauty?"

I swallowed hard, hormones still raging through my body. Stepping back from him, I took a deep breath. "I went to Michigan to confront the man who raped me."

Reed's eyes widened. "Ivy, are you nuts? You went alone?"

I nodded, putting a hand up to quiet him. "Please don't say anything. Let me get this out. It's not what you think."

He took a deep breath, visibly trying to calm himself. "I'm sorry. Go ahead."

A sick taste rose in my throat and I swallowed it. "The man I went to confront . . . who raped me . . . and fathered Noah, is my father."

It wasn't just my voice, but my entire body, that shook as I made the admission. Reed just stared at me, his expression frozen in shock.

"Your . . . father?" he finally said. "He's the one who raped you?"

After a single nod, all the pent-up worry of the past

few months came pouring out. "I didn't want anyone to know. Not just for me, but for Noah, too. I don't want people thinking he's some kind of freak. I wanted to tell you, I did . . . and I should have, before we slept together, because—"

"No." He rested his hands on my shoulders. "Ivy, no. You *never* had to tell me. I'm glad you did, though."

I took a deep breath, gathering my courage. "I was a virgin when it happened."

"Holy shit." His eyes widened. "One man. You told me there'd only been one and . . . God, I'm so sorry. And then there was no one after . . . until . . ."

"Until you."

His face was pained as he ran a hand through his hair and looked up at the ceiling. "It means a lot to me that you trust me with this. But it doesn't change anything between us. I love you with no strings attached."

I blinked and tears poured down both my cheeks. "You still love me?"

"Of course I do. More than ever. I knew you were a survivor, but . . ." He ran a hand through his hair again, "I had no idea, Ivy. How you could be so strong after something like that . . ."

"I'm not strong, though." I grabbed his forearms and held on. "It's been this pressure inside of me that just built and built. And the trial—"

Reed closed his eyes and leaned his forehead against mine. "I'm sorry. That must've been so damn hard for you."

"It was at first. I know how irrational I was, Reed, but in my messed-up mind it was like you were standing up for my father. And that was wrong."

"Anyone would've had trouble coping with that,

Beauty. Did you have anyone to talk to about it?"

I shook my head. "I didn't want anyone to know. I think my friend April suspects, but she's never pushed me to talk about it. I went to a counselor when I first moved to Lovely, but when it came time to talk about it . . . I couldn't. I want to go see her again."

"Good." Reed pulled back and met my eyes. "Listen to me. I love you, and nothing will change that."

"Does it bother you that Noah's father is—"

He cut in. "No. It . . . honestly, Ivy it just . . . makes me want to adopt him even more than I already did."

"Noah?" More tears slipped from my eyes. "You want to adopt him?"

"I was hoping to when we . . . but then you . . . ."

"You mean . . . ." My mouth dropped open. "Really?"

"Yes."

I threw my arms around his neck and he picked me up. My legs instinctively wrapped around his waist. He kissed me, hard and deep. I kissed him back with the same hunger, biting at his lower lip as he walked us over to his open breakfast bar and backed me against the counter.

Everything else was forgotten as we tore at each other's clothes. He kissed and nipped at my neck urgently.

"Here," I said, shoving down the waistband of his jeans. "Take me right here. Right now."

He sighed against my neck. "I can't."

"Yes, you can."

"I've got no self-control right now, Ivy. I'm crazy with wanting you. But don't worry."

He grabbed the sides of my panties and worked them off, bending down to put his face between my thighs.

"No," I said firmly. "I want you inside me. Right now. Please, Reed."

"I don't want to be rough with you."

"Be rough. I need it right now. Don't hold back." I gave him a frantic look. "Condom?"

"I've got one in my wallet."

He took it out, opened it with his teeth and rolled it on.

"At least let me take you to bed," he said, kissing me.

"Right here," I said, moaning as he squeezed my ass in his palms.

Our bodies connected in a swirl of sensation. When he entered me in one powerful thrust, I cried out and rocked my hips against his.

No matter what he gave me, I wanted more. He hammered himself into me and I begged him to do it harder. I was overcome with emotion for him, my eyes meeting his as I came hard, his name coming out of my throat in a scream.

His body tensed and he groaned deeply against my neck. "Ivy," he breathed.

I wrapped myself around him and we stayed that way, breathing each other in, until he carried me to the bedroom and we laid down together.

The peace that surrounded me was complete and perfect. It wasn't too late. I hadn't lost him. I promised myself I'd never take him for granted again.

THE NEXT MORNING, I woke up to the feel of Reed's warm breath on my neck. He was wrapped around me, his chest to my back, our legs tangled together. The closeness was more than physical. I'd opened my soul to him last night, and he'd accepted all of me.

I shifted slightly, hoping to sneak out of bed to the bathroom. Reed tightened his hold around my waist and kissed my shoulder.

"Don't get up," he said, his voice gravelly.

"I have to pee, though."

"Make it quick. I want to spend all morning right here with you."

I turned to face him. "Would it be okay if we went to Margie and Gene's? I'm missing Noah after two nights away from him."

"Yeah, of course."

I stepped out of bed and searched the floor for my shirt.

"Living room," Reed said, giving me a lazy smile.

"Oh. Right." I started to walk that way but stopped in the doorway and turned to face him. "Thanks for . . . understanding, Reed. For giving us another chance."

"I'm in love with you," he said. "I'm not sure you get what that means just yet. It means I'll never give up on us. I'd do anything for you. Love's got ups and downs, and I'm all in, Ivy. I hope you are, too."

"I am. I never want to be without you again."

He smiled at me and stepped out of bed. I turned toward the living room, knowing even one good long look at his body would result in me ending up back in bed with him.

We both showered and dressed and Reed drove us to Margie and Gene's. I'd missed the leathery smell of his truck and the way he looked driving it. My man was rugged, and God, did I love it.

After we parked, Reed opened my door and we walked up to the front door hand in hand. When I saw Margie standing there waiting for us, I was expecting a happy outburst about seeing us back together. But her expression was drawn, the lines by her eyes more pronounced.

"What's going on?" I asked, my heart rate picking up speed. "Margie, is Noah okay?"

"He's fine. It's . . . there's something else I need to tell you."

"What is it?"

Reed wrapped his arm around my waist from behind and I laid my hand over his.

"Maybe we should go sit down," Margie said.

"No, tell me," I said. "Please just tell me."

She sighed and gave me an apologetic look. "Walter Grieves passed away last night."

"Walter?" My heart dropped into my stomach.

"His assistant found him this morning. It looks like he had a stroke."

Reed wrapped his other arm around my waist and pulled me close, my back to his chest. Tears welled in my eyes as I thought about grouchy, particular, kindhearted Walter being gone. He hadn't come in as usual last week, but I figured he was working on a book, or maybe that he'd gone to New York to see his agent as he sometimes did. Now we'd never have another heart to heart conversation. He'd never see me working to become a better writer.

"I don't even know what to say," I said softly, wiping the corners of my eyes.

"I know you were very fond of him," Margie said. "And he was fond of you, too. That's saying something coming from Walter."

I smiled through my tears. "He's actually very big-hearted . . . or, he *was*, I guess."

"It's a real shame." Margie looked up at Reed, acknowledging him for the first time since we'd arrived. "Good to see you, Reed. Would you two like some breakfast?"

"Did Gene make pancakes?" I asked.

"He and Noah are working on them now. Come on in and sit down."

I stepped out of Reed's arms and Margie rubbed a hand over my back.

"Everything went okay on your trip?" she asked me, still wearing a concerned expression.

"Yeah. I've needed to do that for a long time, and I'm relieved it's over."

She nodded silently and we walked into the kitchen where Noah jumped down from his stool, squealing with excitement. He raced toward me and I was about to open my arms when he passed me by and flew into Reed's arms instead.

"Hey, big guy," Reed said, sweeping Noah off the floor and hugging him close.

I'd almost ruined things by making our threesome into a twosome. But now that Reed was back in our lives, I wasn't going to make that mistake again.

SEVERAL DAYS LATER, I sat near the back of the crowded courtroom, waiting to hear the verdict on the trial. It was noon, but the diner had been nearly empty and everyone with any interest in the trial was either packed inside the courtroom or waiting outside on the sidewalk.

No matter what the verdict was, it wouldn't affect my relationship with Reed. I felt lighter since the confrontation with my father. Facing him head-on had helped me stop projecting my resentment onto others.

The courtroom silenced as the bailiff passed the judge a folded piece of paper and he read it before folding it back up and giving it to the bailiff, who handed it to the jury foreman.

Reed and Chuck Ashley stood and then the judge addressed the foreman, "As to the charge of sexual assault, how does the jury find the defendant?"

"Guilty, your honor."

A wave of gasps and whispers swept through the crowd and the judge held up a hand.

"Quiet, please."

The courtroom went silent and the judge continued reading the list of charges, the jury foreman announcing a guilty verdict after each one.

A wave of emotion swelled inside me. I wanted to scream with happiness, but my eyes went to Reed who stood straight and still. I could see from his profile that his face was completely neutral. Chuck Ashley's head was in his hands.

Reed whispered something in Chuck's ear before the bailiff came over and led Chuck away. Reed shook the prosecutor Mark's hand and turned to the crowd, scanning it. He stopped when his eyes locked with mine.

I held his gaze for a few seconds before turning and filing out of the courtroom with everyone else.

"Hope that bastard gets his in prison," a woman murmured to someone.

It was all I could do not tell her she should focus her hopes on Chloe. She was only a sophomore in high school, and she had a long road ahead of her. This trial had been entertainment to some of these people, which was sad and pathetic. We were here because a girl had been victimized by her own stepfather and now she needed the support of the community more than ever.

My emotions swirled, calming by the time I got back to the diner. Margie looked at me stoically.

"You heard?" I asked.

She nodded and opened her arms to me. I let her hold me close.

"How you doin'?" she asked softly.

"I'm okay. Good. Glad it went the way it did."

"Well, I want you to take the rest of the day off. Just take some time—"

Her voice trailed off and I turned to see what she was looking at. Reed was walking through the diner's front door, his tie loosened and his expression relaxed for the first time in a while.

I left Margie's arms and went to him, taking in his scent as he pulled me against the hard lines of his chest.

"You okay?" I whispered in his ear, tightening my arms around his shoulders.

"Yeah. You?"

"I'm alright. Can we step outside?"

He let go of me and took my hand, leading me out to the bench we'd been sitting on the first time he asked me out. For a minute, we just sat, my hand in his lap as he ran his thumb over my knuckles.

"This is awkward," I finally said. "I feel like I should say I'm sorry because you lost, but—"

He squeezed my hand and let out a single note of laughter. "I don't really take it like that. I worked my ass off on that case. I gave Chuck the best defense I was capable of. That was all I could do."

"But are you disappointed?"

He shook his head slightly. "The evidence was solid. And Mark did a good job with it."

"So did you. I was a little pissed at you a couple times during your closing argument, so I think that means you were doing a good job."

Reed let go of my hand and wrapped his arm around my shoulders, pulling me against him.

"I love you so much," he said, kissing my temple.

"I love you, too."

"Yeah? Not pissed at me anymore, then?"

"No."

"I think we need to talk about getting an arrest made in your case. The statute of limitations isn't up. You don't have to decide now, and I support whatever decision you make."

I leaned back so I could meet his gaze. "I've been thinking about it. I want to do that."

"Good. I can make contact with the state police in Michigan. I think they'll take the case since he's a police officer."

I nestled myself against his chest again. "Kind of funny that the strength of a sixteen-year-old girl ended up being my wakeup call."

"We all walk different paths, Beauty. You're the strongest person I've ever known."

His words, and my decision to move ahead with charges against my father, filled me with a sense of peace. Hiding from the truth had been my means of coping for a long time, but I was ready to face it now. And not facing it alone made all the difference.

TWENTY-ONE

A COUPLE BLISSFUL MONTHS passed after the trial. Reed, Noah and I were nearly inseparable. When the ground thawed and spring started making an appearance, we'd walk to the park from Reed's apartment after dinner every evening, with Snoop in tow.

Noah still spent every Friday night with Margie and Gene. Reed and I often spent those nights in bed with a bottle of wine and no worries about how loud we were being.

Charges had been filed against my father, and he was free on bail while his attorney worked on a plea deal. I was relieved, because while I'd been prepared to testify in a trial, his guilty plea made things much easier. Reed was following the case closely, and he kept me updated.

Today I was making the short walk to a downtown law office to meet another Lovely attorney, Dan Stegall. Dan had business he wanted to discuss with me, and Reed was meeting me there. When I'd received an official letter from Dan requesting a meeting I'd freaked out and told Reed I was sure my dad was suing me for visitation with Noah, or defamation of character or some other non-sense.

Despite his assurances that no attorney would take that case, I had a nagging fear in the back of my mind. Life was absolutely perfect right now, almost too good to be true, and I was scared that it would change.

Dan's office had plain white walls and was filled with utilitarian furniture that gave off a sterile smell. I liked the faint smell of books in Reed's office much better. As soon as I walked in, a receptionist greeted me.

"Miss Gleason? Mr. Lockhart is catching up with Mr. Stegall now," she said, leading me down a short hallway.

"Maggie, please call me Ivy. I know I'm here on business but I'm still plain old Ivy," I said. Maggie was one of my regular customers at the diner.

"Sorry," she said, wrinkling her nose. "Work habits die hard. Go on in, Ivy."

"Hey, babe," Reed said, standing up when I walked in.

"Ivy, nice to formally meet you," Dan said, standing up to shake my hand.

"You, too."

"Okay, let's get to it," he said, sitting back down behind his desk. It was impeccably clean, with only one file on the polished dark wood surface. Reed's desk was always filled with stacks of books, files and papers. I loved it when I walked into his office and he looked up at me from behind his desk, wearing his reading glasses.

"So, Ivy, this would normally just be a meeting between you and I . . . unless Mr. Lockhart is your counsel?"

I glanced at Reed and he winked at me.

"Something like that," I said, smiling.

"Excellent. In that case, I've called you here to tell

you that you are the sole recipient of the estate of Walter Grieves."

My mouth fell open and I gave Reed an incredulous look. "Me?"

Dan nodded. "Yes, and it's a significant estate. I've been closing things out as per Mr. Grieves' request, but he hardly owed anyone anything. I had to negotiate a few things with his publisher, but we've concluded our business and everything is in order."

My heart pounded as I took in the news. I pictured Walter sitting next to me on the bench in the park that day, wearing his hat and trench coat, telling me I should feel like a survivor. Tears welled in my eyes and I broke down in tears.

"I'm sorry," I said. Reed put an arm around my shoulders and I leaned against him.

"It shouldn't be me," I said. "He hardly knew me."

"Walter was a very private man," Dan said. "I'm not sure anyone knew him well. He didn't have any family when he died."

I thought about the daughter he'd lost and shook my head sadly.

"He thought a lot of you, Ivy," Dan said. "He was very clear about what he wanted. He instructed me to give you this letter from him, liquidate anything you don't want from the estate and pay all proceeds to you."

"Liquidate . . . you're selling his things?"

Dan nodded. "The house, his vehicles and his personal property. I'm planning an estate sale."

"I want his books. And his computer. Anything related to his writing, I want to keep."

"Sure thing."

"How much are we talking here, Dan?" Reed asked.

Dan looked down at a paper on his desk. "Without the estate sale proceeds it's a little over eighteen million."

I sat back in my chair, shock rendering me speechless.

"Wow," Reed said. "Ivy, this is amazing."

"I don't . . . I can't even . . ."

"Take some time to let this sink in," Dan said. "In the meantime, here's the letter he asked me to give you."

He passed me a blank white envelope and I looked down at it and tucked it into my purse.

"Would you like me to work with your counsel from here on out?" Dan asked, grinning as he glanced between Reed and me.

"That would be great, Dan," I said, taking the hand Reed held out to me.

Now that the preliminary meeting was concluded Reed and I said goodbye to Dan and walked outside. I headed for a nearby metal bench where I sat down and opened the letter from Walter.

Dear Ivy,

I'm most disappointed to be dead. I had so many more books to write and dishes of oatmeal to eat. But it wasn't meant to be, apparently.

I guess by now you know I'm leaving everything to you. Being able to do so is one of the greatest pleasures of my life. You're much more to me than daily breakfast company. Your hard work and devotion to your son remind me just how strong and resilient the human spirit is.

Do amazing things with this money. Travel. Have fun. Finish that degree. Most importantly, write. In some measure, it makes me feel like you'll be finishing what I can't.

All my best on living your dreams.

Walter

I was crying hard by the time I finished reading. I passed the letter to Reed and he held me against his chest as he read it himself.

"Wow," he said. "You do leave quite the impression, Miss Gleason. I have to agree with him there. You deserve this."

"But . . . it's just so unexpected. I don't know what to do with that kind of money."

"Don't do anything with it until you're ready. Keep going to work every day and living life as usual. With time, you'll know what to do. I can help get a trust set up for Noah, and you'll need a will immediately."

"Will everyone in Lovely hear about it?" I asked.

"No. Dan is bound to keep this information confidential. And you and I won't be telling people about it right now. That's important, Ivy. People will come knocking on your door if they hear. I don't want you in danger. Word will get out eventually, but for now let's keep it to ourselves."

"No, I won't say anything to anyone. At least not now."

Reed's face fell with disappointment.

"What?" I put a hand on his knee.

"I was planning to propose to you before long, and I don't want it to come off like I did it because of the money."

I laughed and cupped his cheeks in my hands. "Reed, I'd never think that."

"We'll have a prenup drawn up."

"We will *not*. What's mine is yours. Now stop talking about paperwork and set your mind to thinking about engagement rings instead."

His eyes softened. "I like the sound of Ivy Lockhart, don't you?"

"Very much. I can hardly wait."

He kissed me and walked me to the diner door before heading back to his office. When I walked in and saw Margie staring up at Springer on the TV screen, I walked behind the counter and pulled her close in a big hug.

"What's this for?" she asked, hugging me back.

"Just for being you."

"Can you believe this guy?" She nodded up at the TV. "Got three different women pregnant in a month. Why would any of those bimbos want him? I'd kick him to the curb."

I took a pastry from the cabinet and bit into it. "Margie,

what would you do if you won the lottery?"

She laughed and shook her head. "No chance of that happening. I don't even play."

"But if you did . . . what would you do?"

"I'd pay for Noah's college. Buy you and him a nice little house with a yard. Replace the roof on our house. And buy Gene a new grill for the kitchen here."

"You wouldn't want to travel somewhere amazing? Or buy a yacht?"

She waved a hand. "We're simple people. Lovely's our home. If we had all those things I mentioned, life would be just about perfect."

I smiled, now knowing the first things I'd do when I got the money. Being able to help the people I loved was an amazing gift in itself. Once again, Walter proved to be the wisest person I'd ever known.

As I sat at the counter eating my pastry I thought about my life. I had so much to be thankful for. Four years ago I never would have dreamed that my life would turn out the way it had. But I was still Ivy Gleason and the things that mattered to me then, still mattered to me now. I had grown and matured and I was proud of everything I had accomplished and knowing that Reed and Margie and Gene and Walter felt the same way about me made my heart full. I was one lucky girl.

THREE MONTHS LATER
REED

I COULD HEAR IVY'S footsteps as she walked down the open wooden staircase of the vacant downtown Lovely house we'd just toured. It was a gem–a renovated century old home with nearly four thousand square feet and five bedrooms. It sat on a nice piece of property and it was a bit of a Lovely landmark.

"It's beautiful, I love it," she said as she walked through the foyer. "But it's awfully big—"

"I was hoping we could fill it up with some more kids," I said. "Noah would make a great big brother. But first you'll need to marry me. What do you say, Beauty?" I was standing in front of the fireplace in the great room, holding a blue Tiffany ring box.

I held my breath as she covered the space between us.

"Yes," she said softly. "I say yes."

Noah ran into the room as I was sliding the ring onto her finger.

"It's shiny!" he cried.

"He's already seen it," I explained to Ivy. "We had a long talk about this."

"Oh, you did, huh?"

"He accepted my proposal to be his Dad. Didn't you, big guy?"

Noah threw his arms around my legs and I felt a swell of love in my heart. Ivy kissed me and then held her hand out to admire the ring.

"It's spectacular," she said.

I'd known the square-cut solitaire with sapphires on the sides was the one as soon as I saw it. The blue stones reminded me of Ivy's eyes.

"I was thinking we could get married this summer," I said, loving the way her hand looked with my ring on it.

"But that's just a couple months away. Can we pull a wedding together so fast?"

"My mom's a miracle worker with these kinds of

things."

"This summer, then." She smiled and ruffled Noah's hair. "Do you want this to be our new home, Noah?"

"Yeah!" he cried, breaking away from my legs and doing a lap around the room.

I pulled Ivy into my arms, marveling that I'd been lucky enough to find her and Noah. And, what's more, lucky enough that they loved me, too.

Life was good. And I had a feeling it would only get better from here on out.

EPILOGUE

Ivy

REED HOISTED NOAH UP on his shoulders so Noah could set the star on top of the Christmas tree. There was a chorus of 'aww' and scattered applause as my son grinned down at us and plopped the star onto the tree.

"Yay!" he cried, throwing his arms in the air.

This was the second Christmas tree we'd decorated today. Reed had chopped both of them down in true lumberjack form, wearing the brown canvas coat I still appreciated seeing him in.

The other tree was sparkling in the front window of our home. This one adorned the front window of Grieves House, the venture I'd thrown my heart and soul into for the past few months.

We'd done all the smart things Reed had suggested

when we got the money from Walter's estate. Having investments and a college fund and trust for Noah helped my husband sleep at night, and I loved that about him.

It had been a thrill when we'd bought Gene's new commercial range and grill, along with new ovens for the diner. He'd grinned for days after they were installed. We'd also had a new roof put on Margie and Gene's house, as well as a sunroom. They were over the moon.

Once we'd taken care of those things, I approached Reed about an idea I'd been thinking about. I wanted to create a safe haven for pregnant teenagers who might not have anywhere else to go. It would be a safe place without judgment. We'd help them get prenatal care, learn how to take care of a baby, and help them get on their feet. From my own experience, I knew how much a young girl, pregnant and alone, needed love and support and encouragement.

With Margie and Gene's blessing I'd quit my job at the diner to start Grieves House, and now I was living a dream. Every time a new girl arrived I knew I'd found my calling.

"When's our new house mom arriving?" Reed asked as he lifted Noah from his shoulders, settling him on his hip. Noah gazed up at him happily.

"April's planning on getting here the day after Christmas," I said. "She's got plans with her family for the holiday but she's anxious to get here and start as soon as she can."

"I can't wait to meet her."

I smiled as I thought about my friend, who'd pulled me up when I needed it most. She'd never felt truly settled in Seattle, and when I'd told her I was looking for a house mom to live at Grieves House, she'd jumped at the chance.

Everything had fallen into place. April was the last member of the new family I'd made for myself, and she was moving to Lovely. She was one of the few people I knew I could trust to help me run Grieves House. My father had pleaded guilty to sexual assault charges in a deal that kept him from prison but meant he'd never work as a police officer again. The prosecutor had approached me about it, and I'd told him I was satisfied. My father had admitted what he did and he wasn't in a position to victimize anyone else through his job. I'd been surprised to get an apologetic email from Levi after the story hit the papers in Lexington. When I'd written back, I'd told him I had no hard feelings, which was true.

Over four years ago I'd been sure my faith in the goodness of people was gone forever. But I'd since learned that while not everyone was inherently good, there were other people whose goodness was so strong it outshone the bad. And I was grateful to be surrounded by that goodness.

Reed wrapped me in his free arm, still holding Noah with his other. I closed my eyes and took in the scents of his cologne and the sweet frosting from the Christmas cookies I'd decorated with Noah this morning. The scents that told me no matter where the three of us were standing right now, we were home.

AUTHOR'S NOTE

THANK YOU SO MUCH for reading Deep Down. If you enjoyed it, I'd greatly appreciate a review at the site of the retailer you purchased it from.

I initially planned this story as a standalone, but my smart and supportive group of three early readers let me know I'd gotten it wrong. They wanted more of the Lockhart brothers, and when they each mentioned it, I got excited about the idea. I look forward to bringing you Mason Lockhart's story next.

ABOUT THE AUTHOR

BRENDA ROTHERT LIVES IN Central Illinois with her husband and three sons. She was a daily print journalist for nine years, during which time she enjoyed writing a wide range of stories.

These days Brenda writes New Adult Romance in the Contemporary and Dystopian genres. She loves to hear from readers.

CONNECT WITH BRENDA

www.brendarothert.com

Facebook

Twitter

Goodreads

Pinterest

ACKNOWLEDGEMENTS

THIS BOOK IS FIRST and foremost dedicated to survivors. Whatever your struggle, you're not alone. Don't be afraid to reach out until you find the support you need. You're worth it.

My village continues to grow, and I'm blessed beyond words to know every person who plays a role in my work, be it big or small. This book challenged me, and I needed more feedback than usual as I wrote it.

For helping me shape my open, I'd like to thank Christine Borgford, Carrie Jones, Pam Million, GP Ching, Stephanie Reid and Karla Sorensen. These women have my back and came to my rescue when I needed it most.

For reading and providing feedback on the entire book, thanks go to Denise Sprung, Janett Gomez, Michelle Tan and M.E. Carter. Their honesty and enthusiasm pushed me when the writing was hard. Thank you hardly seems enough for what they've all done for me.

Editor Valerie Gray partnered with me to bring this book to life. From concept to completion, she was there every step of the way. She didn't just share my excitement, but also my frustration and anxiety over whether I could do this story justice. And her attention to detail is just scary good.

Christine Borgford of Perfectly Publishable is more than just a formatter. She came to the rescue when I needed her, encouraged me and listened to me when I needed it. And when it comes to formatting, she's the best.

My assistant Pam Million is one in a . . . um, you see where I'm going with this, don't you? She's there through the ups and downs. A friend who gets your crazy and stays around is a friend indeed. Everyone should have a Pam in their life. But not my Pam. You'll have to find your own. (Sorry.)

Speaking of awesome Pams, Pam Carrion has infused new life into my social media. Her energy and optimism make me smile every day.

Rosarita Reader is my beta reader extraordinaire. MWAH!

The members of Rothert's Readers are my constant support of friendship and inspiration. I'm so grateful for every one of them.

To the many bloggers who work so hard at what you do simply for love of books, thank you. I wouldn't be here without you.

My husband and three boys are my biggest motivation. You may have noticed that family plays an important role in my books. That's because my family reminds me every day that truly, nothing matters more.

42388311R00146

Made in the USA
Charleston, SC
24 May 2015